Sky Girl and the Superheroic Adventures

Joe Sergi

Martin Sisters Publishing

For Yee and Lizzie,
My Real Sky Girls

CHAPTER 0

Fourteen years ago

Dianne Dandrudge Christopher sat in the second-floor nursery of 16 Hartland Court. The rain poured outside, and Dianne could hear the drops as they pounded against the windows of the nursery. The wind whistled as it blew through the roof.

A loud grumble startled the sixteen-month-old girl sitting on Dianne's lap. "It's okay, baby. Just a little thunder," Dianne cooed to the young girl. To further distract her daughter, Dianne pointed to the picture of a bright red fire truck that jutted from the page of the pop-up book she was reading to the young girl.

The girl tried to sound out the words and said, "Feer trook."

Dianne smiled. "Very good, DeDe."

The doorbell rang.

"Your father probably forgot his house key again." Dianne stood up to answer it. "You stay here and read and Mommy will get the door."

DeDe responded, "Momma?"

"Shush, I'll be right back." Dianne smiled as she left the room. She walked down the hall and closed the childproof gate.

DeDe turned the page. A smiling yellow Volkswagen protruded from the pop-up book. DeDe smiled. "Punshbooggie." Proud of herself, she got up to follow her mother down the hall and share her discovery.

DeDe soon reached the large gate at the end of the hall. Standing on her tiptoes, the child spied her mother at the bottom of the stairs. She could see two men there, a fireman and a policeman, talking to her mother.

DeDe yelled down the stairs at the three people. "DaDa?"

And her mother burst into tears.

"No, honey." Dianne sobbed as she walked up the stairs. Dianne picked her daughter up as tears streamed down her face. "DaDa's not coming home tonight."

DeDe did not understand. Not then, not through the funeral, nor at the cemetery. In fact, it took several years for her to realize that her father was not coming home ever again.

CHAPTER 1

The Present

Nick Long made the long walk home from Wall Street to his small studio apartment at 295 Greenwich Street. His apartment was located in the section of Manhattan referred to as the Triangle Below Canal, Tribeca for short. Nick knew he paid far too much rent for less than six hundred square feet of apartment. But that was life in the big city.

As he did every night, Nick walked up Broadway and made a right on Chambers Street. He could see the lights of Ground Zero in the distance highlighting the spot where the twin towers fell on 9/11. The sight of construction trucks in the distance gave him a sense of pride. The city was already rebuilding on the land.

Nick rounded the corner and passed by City Hall Park. As he crossed Chambers street, he heard a noise in the bushes in front of the park. Out of the corner of his eye, Nick was sure that he saw something move in the dark trees. He picked up his pace. As he did, Nick looked over his shoulder and stared into the park, hoping to catch a glimpse of what he heard.

Nick was still staring into the park when he collided with the teenage girl wearing a long trench coat.

The girl did not fall. Instead, Nick felt as if he had slammed into a brick wall. Stunned and winded, the burly man tumbled backwards to the ground.

The red-haired girl gave a shy smile and extended a gloved hand to Nick.

Nick took her hand and looked up at the newcomer. Her five-foot frame stood confident on the dark street. The teenage girl was pretty and wore a brown trench coat, though the temperature was nearly ninety-five degrees on this hot August night. Nick looked closer to see that she wasn't even sweating. Despite the trench coat, Nick could see that she was wearing purple boots and gloves. He gave her a friendly smile.

The teen's smile widened, and her blue eyes glinted in the lamp light.

The two stared at each other for a second, and then the girl spoke. "So, um, are you going to get up or what?"

Nick realized he was staring at her. "Sorry. I didn't expect anyone to be out here." He held on to her hand and she easily pulled him to his feet. "I'm okay. I guess I was just a little nervous, what with the recent rise in crime and all. I didn't want to be caught by surprise."

"Good job with that." The teen winked at him as she mocked him. "I'm sure falling down was all part of your plan."

"More or less," Nick added with a grin.

Just then, Nick heard a noise in the bushes again. He spun toward the sound, turning away from the girl. Nick squinted into the darkness and watched as four large, hulking figures emerged from the bushes in the park. With a growl, the attackers rushed toward him.

"You have to get out of here!" Nick turned back to warn the teen.

But she was gone.

Nick stood alone and confused in the center of Chambers Street.

His confusion was soon replaced by fear as one of the figures from the park tackled him. The impact knocked Nick to the ground again. This time, when he looked up, he did not see an attractive teen. The stockbroker rubbed his eyes and looked again.

The creatures were still there: four large silverback apes dressed in army green camouflage uniforms. The largest one moved toward him and growled, revealing its sharp fangs.

Nick threw his hands over his head and closed his eyes.

There was a loud thud, and he opened his eyes just in time to see the large ape fly through the air and back into the park. Nick heard someone behind him say, in a deep woman's baritone, "Didn't anyone tell you it's not nice to eat people?"

The well-dressed executive turned around to see someone floating a foot above the sidewalk. Nick recognized her as the girl that had helped him mere minutes ago. Only now, she wore a purple mask over her blue eyes and had removed her trench coat, revealing a black spandex body suit, which accentuated her muscular frame. A matching purple cape, gloves, boots, and skirt completed the girl's costume. The skirt was emblazoned with a silver molecular symbol on it. Nick immediately recognized the symbol as belonging to the comic book character known as SkyBoy. "Whoa."

Nick watched as the girl slowly floated to the ground. She brushed a strand of red hair from her face. "Okay, Gorilla Army, time for round two." She flew into the remaining three creatures, scattering them like bowling pins.

As if on cue, the fourth ape exited the woods with a large rifle. Nick tried to warn the girl, but he was too late. The weapon fired an energy bolt that slammed into her and sent her crashing towards the ground.

Nick watched as the girl executed a perfect tuck and roll before hitting the grass. Nick exhaled in relief as the costumed girl easily regained her footing.

"I think it's time for a SkyPulse!" she exclaimed as she extended her hands toward the ape. The weapon burst into flames, igniting the gorilla's fur. The panicked creature dove into the City Hall fountain in an attempt to extinguish himself. Smoke rose from the water. The smell of burnt fur filled the air.

The teen gave Nick an innocent look. "Whoops!"

With a smile, the girl turned back to the other three apes. Faster than Nick's eyes could see, she grabbed a heavy support net from a nearby construction site and wrapped up the remaining apes. With little effort, she tossed the creatures across the park and into the pond, trapping the fourth ape with them.

When the battle was over, the young girl hovered above the park and surveyed the situation. She slowly floated to the ground in front of Nick.

Nick could hear her talking. "What are you talking about? My banter was not hackneyed! C'mon. 'Time for SkyPulse?' That was great!"

"What?" Nick asked before he noticed the wireless headset. "Hold on. I gotta check on the guy." For the second time that evening, she extended her hand to Nick to help him to his feet.

"Um, thanks," Nick stammered. "Was I just attacked by monkeys in combat gear?"

The girl smiled. "They were apes. Monkeys have tails. Everybody knows that. Make sure to tell the police that these apes are really smart, so they should send them to jail and not put them in a zoo or something. "

Nick just stared at the girl. "That was amazing."

She blushed and then spoke into the headset. "What? I'm not going to say that. Why? Because it's dumb." There was a long pause, and finally the girl said, "Fine, you win. I'll do it." She turned to Nick and added quietly, "It was all in a night's work." She listened for a moment and then mumbled the word, "Citizen."

The costumed teen started to fly away. Before she could get too far off the ground, Nick grabbed her arm. He could feel the muscles in her small but compact triceps. "Wait. Who are you?"

The girl turned back to him and placed her hands on her hips. "Me? I'm Sky Girl, silly." She slowly began to float off the ground. "And you should be more careful at night. I wouldn't want to see a cutie like you get hurt. Bye bye."

With that, Sky Girl flew away.

Nick watched as she disappeared into the night sky in a blur of black and purple. After a few moments, he finally shook his head and said, "Good golly!"

CHAPTER 2

Meanwhile, an hour south in a small New Jersey suburb called Colonia, Jason Shewstal sat at a computer in the lower level of 16 Hartland Court. The lanky teen adjusted his headset as he stared at the computer monitor, then fidgeted with his jeans, which were even more wrinkled than usual. Jason yanked down on his red T-shirt. The shirt had a burn hole in it below the words, *I went on an away mission and all I got was this lousy t-shirt.*

Jason was not happy.

Jason took a deep breath and spoke into the headset, "'A cutie?' We do not refer to the people we rescue as 'cuties.' We call them citizens or ma'am or sir." He listened to the response through the headset and sighed. "You should come home anyway. We have school tomorrow. Plus, I smell your mom's lasagna."

Jason took off his headset and sighed again. "'Cutie,' indeed." A gust of wind blew Jason's messy blond hair. He got up and opened the large glass door that led from the basement into the fenced-in backyard.

Sky Girl flew in through the open glass door to the basement. "But he was a cutie!" The heroine smiled as she took off her purple mask, revealing the face of Jason's best friend, Deirdre "DeDe" Christopher. She slowly slid the glass door closed. It made a low whump as it connected with the doorframe. DeDe winced at the noise.

"Shhh. Your mom will hear. What took you so long? Did you get lost again?" Jason asked with a smile.

DeDe pouted. "I did not get lost. I had to go back for my trench coat. After that, I followed the parkway until I got home. No problem."

Jason smiled. "A brilliant idea."

"If you say so, Mr. Smarty Pants," she chided.

DeDe walked over to the corner of the room and looked into the full-length mirror. "I just wish the costume wasn't so, I don't know . . ." She lifted her cape to look at her rear end in the mirror. "Tight."

"I had not noticed," Jason squeaked as he forced himself to look back at the computer screen. DeDe smiled. Jason never used contractions and spoke in perfect grammar, even when he was flummoxed.

"Well I'd better 'check in' before dinner," DeDe said, making finger quotes in the air.

Jason turned away from the computer and watched as DeDe walked over to the purple yoga mat in the corner on the basement and sat in a cross-legged position. Jason knew full well who she had to "check in" with and found the whole concept fascinating. "Get me a souvenir."

"Nice. Be right back." DeDe closed her eyes and concentrated.

* * *

When DeDe opened her eyes again, she was no longer in her Colonia basement. Instead, she stood in the center of a large council chamber.

DeDe thought about the first time she had stood in this ornate room. It was just after the gymnastics-dance semi-finals. She remembered her confusion at being able to see through the gymnasium wall during her dance routine and then again when she vaulted herself through the gymnasium ceiling after the competition. But neither of those events could compare to what had occurred when DeDe had closed her eyes to go to sleep and awoke in this chamber, the headquarters of the Galactic Protectorate. The Protectorate was made up of a group of alien creatures who wanted DeDe to accept the mantle of SkyBoy. After some initial hesitation, and with the help of her best friend Jason, DeDe accepted her destiny and took them up on their offer. She became Sky Girl. She had spent much of the summer trying to master her powers.

"Miss Christopher? Is there something we can help you with?" The soft voice brought DeDe back to reality. She turned toward the head table at the front of the room and the source of the voice. An older woman with the head of a lizard sat in between two other alien creatures: an owl woman and a ferret man. DeDe knew these aliens well. They were the Council of the Galactic Protectorate.

Sky Girl's bosses.

"Hey Boosadah. Wassup?" DeDe gave a large smile to the lizard woman and pointed at the alien with both fingers.

Boosadah, the lizard woman, tried to hide her smile. The ferret man DeDe knew as Woolish grunted in disgust. "No respect."

DeDe got the hint and straightened her posture to her full five-foot height. "Sorry, Woolish. Sky Girl reporting in."

Boosadah adjusted her chair and spoke with an air of authority, "And what is your report, Sky Girl? The Council of the Galactic Protectorate will now recognize and hear you."

15

DeDe smiled. *"Well, after searching all summer, Jason and I finally found Commander Chimp's Gorilla army. They were hiding out in a park in Tribeca, New York."*

"That makes sense since it was near . . ." the owl woman, Peifei said, but then Boosadah gave her a sharp glance. Peifei stopped herself. When she next spoke, it was with annoyance. *"And I assume that you apprehended them?"*

DeDe beamed. *"Apprehend them? Did I ever, Peifei. First there was a slam, and then one of them shot at me—KPEWW—but I pulsed his butt with a TWOO TWOO. Then I wrapped them all up in construction netting with a WHOOSH."* The teenager danced around the room, recreating the fight in an elaborate pantomime.

Woolish, the Ferret man, sighed. *"Such excitement. The legacy ees just like her father—ees no self-control."*

Seeing an opening, DeDe whipped around to Woolish and asked, *"About that? I was wondering if you would tell me more about my father."* Over the summer, DeDe had learned many times that she could not force the Protectorate to talk about her dad.

Woolish shifted uncomfortably and turned to give Boosadah a questioning look.

Boosadah's red eyes softened. *"Soon, Deirdre. Soon. It is not time yet."*

A loud noise erupted from the rear of the chamber. DeDe turned to see the crowd part and a large hulking rock-like creature rush towards her through the opening.

The creature yelled, *"GRONK!"* DeDe winced as she braced for impact. Large rocky arms gathered her up, embracing her in a bear hug that squeezed the teen.

Boosadah made a small, almost imperceptible, smile at the sight.

"I missed you too, Gronk." DeDe said as she returned the hug. *"Good thing I'm invulnerawhatsits or these Gronk-sized hugs would really hurt."*

The pair released their embrace. The rock creature grunted again and handed DeDe a stack of comic books. "Thanks, big guy. Jason will love these." DeDe took the books and turned toward the council. "Well, I'd better get going. I start school tomorrow, so I'm going to be busy."

Boosadah nodded. "Concentrate on your studies, Deirdre."

"Uh, yeah, that's what I meant." DeDe smiled. "Don't worry. I'll try to check in soon."

She bowed, closed her eyes, and concentrated.

* * *

DeDe opened her eyes. She could see that Jason had moved within inches of her face and was sticking his tongue out at her. She giggled. "Nice. Real mature."

Jason gestured to the books that had appeared in DeDe's hands. "So?" he asked, his brown eyes beaming. "What did you get me?"

She handed him Gronk's books. The comic geek closely examined each one before carefully placing it in its own mylar plastic bag with acetate backing board. DeDe watched her best friend with a devious smile as he performed his task with military precision.

When all the books were catalogued and stored, Jason looked up, smiled, and said, "Gronk is awesome!"

DeDe put her finger up and was about to mock him when Jason added, "And Shut up!"

They both laughed. Then there was a knock on the door. DeDe became a blur as she rushed into the closet in her Sky Girl costume. A second later, she emerged in pink sweats and a t-shirt from the Broadway production of Cats. Jason nodded approvingly. "You are certainly getting good at the quick change. Nice shirt."

"Now and forever," DeDe read off her shirt as she walked to the door.

DeDe opened the door to reveal her mother, Dianne, standing in the doorway. Dianne smiled as she wiped her hands with a dish towel. "Are you kids going to stay down here all night? I made dinner."

Although Jason did not possess DeDe's amazing SkySpeed, he easily beat her up the stairs to the kitchen table.

CHAPTER 3

After dinner was over, DeDe and Jason cleared the table. The pair stood at the sink as DeDe washed the dishes and Jason dried.

Dianne, still at the table, leaned back in her chair and smiled. "You know, a mother could get used to this." She put her feet up on another chair.

Jason turned around to look at Dianne. "If you keep making lasagna, Mrs. C., I will wash all the dishes in the house."

DeDe nudged him. "Such a kiss-up."

Dianne laughed as she turned back to the table and picked up a newspaper. "So are you two ready for school tomorrow? You know things are never going to be the same again. Are you nervous about beginning a great adventure with your newfound identity?"

Jason dropped a dish.

Before the dish could hit the floor, DeDe scooped it up at SkySpeed. As she passed Jason the plate, he gave her a worried look.

DeDe tried to appear unconcerned, but her voice still quavered. "New identity, Mom? What new identity?"

"You're a junior now. That's very different than being a sophomore." Dianne put down the paper and moved her feet to the floor. She put her hands on her chin and leaned on the table. Her eyes watered. "My little girl is growing up."

DeDe exhaled in relief. "I'm sure we'll adjust." She smiled as she put her hands on her mother's shoulders. A strand of red hair fell into DeDe's face. "And don't worry, mother dear. I'm not a grown-up yet—you're still stuck with me for a little while," she said and blew the strand of red hair away from her face.

Dianne put her hand on DeDe's. "Then I guess I won't convert the basement into an exercise room after all." Dianne smiled as she stood up and approached the sink. "Speaking of that, I just don't understand what you guys have been doing cooped up in the basement every night for the whole summer."

Jason had been expecting this question. "DeDe told me that her dad, Mr. Christopher, wrote the SkyBoy comic books, and I've been sharing my collection with her."

"Well, that's very nice, Jason." Dianne patted him on the back, and the lanky teen blushed.

Jason's mind wandered. He could never tell her the real reason they were down there. He did not mention that SkyBoy was real but that, thanks to an evil machine created by Professor Z and Evil Brain, the teen superhero had been wiped from existence. Even worse, no one aside from a handful of people remembered that there ever was a real SkyBoy. As far as the world was concerned, SkyBoy was merely a fictional character created by Donald Davis.

Then, last year, DeDe began to develop powers similar to SkyBoy's. With Jason's help, she learned to deal with her newfound powers, and the Galactic Protectorate revealed that SkyBoy was real. But there was still the mystery of why DeDe had inherited his powers.

That answer came from DeDe's mother, Dianne, who revealed that Donald Davis was the pen name of Cain Christopher—DeDe's late father. It all made sense. Her father must have been SkyBoy. Jason realized that it would have been easy for him to write the comic books from his own memories of his adventures. What he didn't know was why. Perhaps her father was trying to provide clues for DeDe in case he disappeared and SkyBoy's enemies returned.

Unfortunately, SkyBoy's enemies had returned—or at least one had. He was Commander Chimp, a mystically enhanced super intelligent chimpanzee who had disguised himself as DeDe and Jason's chemistry teacher. Commander Chimp had tried to trick DeDe into winning him a mystical trophy called the Choyut Dragon so he could use it in his plan to take over the world. When it became clear that DeDe was not going to win the Dragon trophy, the villain called upon MechApe, a sixty-foot mechanical monster, to take the Choyut Dragon by force. Luckily, Sky Girl had been able to stop Commander Chimp and defeat MechApe with the help of her coach, Samantha Lee. In an even stranger turn of events, Coach Lee had turned out to be a tiger woman from the Choyut Village. Before it was all over, Jason had nearly been killed, and the gymnasium had been destroyed in the battle.

Shortly thereafter, DeDe decided to officially adopt the Sky Girl identity. The two of them had spent the summer training. He could barely believe what had happened himself; there was no way Dianne would believe him. It was too amazing. He smiled.

DeDe tapped the side of Jason's head, snapping him back to reality. "Earth to Jason?"

"Sorry, I was thinking about—" He looked at Dianne and smiled. "—our adventures."

DeDe smiled back. "Now you're just babbling. Listen, you look wasted. You'd better go home and get to bed; we have a big day tomorrow."

"So everyone tells me." Jason hugged his friend.

DeDe watched as he walked down the stairs from the kitchen and out the door of 16 Hartland Court. DeDe concentrated on using her SkyVision and continued to watch Jason's heat signature as he walked the rest of the way home.

A few minutes later, DeDe walked down the stairs and into her room. She crawled into her bed under her purple comforter and looked up at the ceiling, "Well, Dad, it's going to be an interesting year. I wish you could be here for it." DeDe turned over on her side and quickly fell asleep.

CHAPTER 4

The next morning, Jason and DeDe walked down the gravel path that led to the Debole Academy. The building had been freshly cleaned for the new school year. Jason made some comment about that "new school" smell, but DeDe did not hear him. Instead, she could only stare at the construction cones cordoning off the area surrounding the remains of the gymnasium. DeDe sulked as they passed the ruins of the structure.

Jason put his hand on his friend's back. "DeDe, for the umpteenth time, it was not your fault that MechApe self-destructed and destroyed the school gymnasium."

DeDe sighed. "I know. I know."

As they approached the main door to the school, the pair walked past a tall, muscular black man, who watched them walk by; his bald head reflected the sunlight as he absentmindedly stroked his goatee. "Miss Christopher, Mr. Shewstal."

"Good morning, Principal Vilbran," Jason said. His voice rose in singsong mock reverence as he imitated the tone of a kindergarten student.

DeDe nudged Jason to be quiet as they entered the doorway. Forcing a smile, she mumbled, "Good morning, sir."

Principal Vilbran sneered back as they entered the lobby. "I am watching you two," he said in a deep baritone.

Once inside, DeDe leaned over and whispered to her best friend, "There's just something about that guy that rubs me the wrong way."

Jason gave a cocky grin, "He is the principal, there is supposed to be something about him that you do not like. Besides, we are really early today and there is not a thing that man can do to us before the first bell." As they rounded the corner, Jason looked to make sure the hallway was empty and that they were alone before he added, "Besides, what are you afraid of? You took out five super-powered gorillas yesterday. I do not think one balding middle management administrator has a chance against you."

DeDe giggled as she took a small purple piece of paper from her backpack. "We better get going if we ever hope to find our new lockers; they're in the West hallway." She pointed down the long corridor that led toward the center of the school.

Jason offered a bow. "Lead on, my lady."

"Dork!" DeDe said as she walked past him.

The pair continued toward their new lockers. When they passed their old chemistry classroom, the name Professor Cornelius, Commander Chimp's secret identity, was still stenciled on the frosted glass of the classroom door. DeDe could not help but think about the evil villain and wondered what happened to Coach Lee.

Sensing DeDe's thoughts, Jason leaned over and whispered, "Coach Lee was a tough tiger lady. I am sure we have seen the last of that evil Chimp."

Before DeDe could respond, a voice called out to them from the hallway. "Hey, DeDe! How was your summer?"

Jason turned to see Adam Berg, a senior. Adam was the school quarterback, held the state football record for the most points scored per game, the all-time passing record, and pretty much everything else. He was tall, muscular, and handsome. He also happened to be DeDe's high school crush.

She gave Adam a warm smile that lit up her entire face, "Hey, summer. My Adam was great. I mean my summer was neat. Lots of stuff. Uh, neat stuff."

"That's, uh, great, DeDe." Adam smiled and DeDe melted inside. "You know, I was a lifeguard at the swim club this summer. I looked for you every day at the pool, but I never saw you."

"Of course you were a lifeguard," Jason muttered under his breath.

DeDe looked at Jason and stammered, "Yeah, I never really made it to the pool. I had other . . . stuff . . . to keep me busy, neat stuff."

Adam smiled wider. "Cool! I just missed you."

Jason muttered under his breath again, "Oh, hi, Adam the lifeguard. My summer was great, too. Thanks for asking."

DeDe elbowed Jason in the ribs, and he grunted before turning to the locker, his back to DeDe and Adam.

DeDe blew on the red strand of hair that had fallen in her face and gave another smile. She began to talk to Adam when she noticed that that someone was walking up behind him. "Yeah, I missed . . ."

DeDe's jaw dropped, and she gasped when she saw who had approached.

"What happened?" Jason asked as he turned around. He followed DeDe's gaze and exclaimed, "Holy plot twist!"

DeDe did not move. She just stared at the girl standing next to Adam. It wasn't just the fact that she was there that shocked DeDe, but also the fact that the brunette was wearing a Debole Academy uniform.

"Deep breaths," Jason whispered, his hands on DeDe's shoulders.

Adam glanced over his shoulder at the new arrival. "Oh, that's right. You guys know each other. Isn't it great?" he said taking the girl's hand. "Nicole Debis was able to transfer here for her senior year."

"Yeah, that's just great," DeDe finally said coldly as she stared at Nicole. "Isn't it great, Jason?" She spoke through gritted teeth.

She had known Nicole all her life, and the two were bitter rivals. Unfortunately, Nicole had more money, more popularity, and as much as DeDe hated to admit it, was a better dancer. She was also, to DeDe's dismay, Adam's girlfriend. DeDe watched with disgust as Nicole leaned in and kissed Adam full on the lips before turning towards them.

Jason thought Adam appeared uncomfortable at Nicole's public display of affection as he slowly moved away from her.

"It is, isn't it?" Nicole said in her usual condescending tone. "Even though I was at the Princeton Academy, Daddy thought I should try to go to school with some non-Princeton students for my senior year. He said it would build character."

DeDe could only stare in response.

The long, uncomfortable silence was broken when Jason gave a loud forced laugh. "Well I am sure that you will have no problem blending with us commoners." DeDe heard that special tone of voice Jason reserved just for Nicole. The three of them had grown up together, and Jason had almost as many reasons as she did to despise Nicole.

Nicole gave Jason an icy glare before she turned and walked away.

Jason turned to Adam and made an exaggerated shrug. "I do not think she likes me. I just have no idea why. Was it something I said?" Jason tried not to smile as he spoke.

Adam turned to DeDe and gave her a pained look. He struggled to say something. DeDe leaned in with interest to hear.

Instead, Adam turned down the hall and chased after Nicole.

Jason turned to DeDe. "Wow. Just...wow. I did not see that coming."

DeDe didn't respond. Instead, she stared in mute shock as she watched Nicole vanish down the hallway with Adam in pursuit. Finally, she forced herself to say, "I can't believe it. Nicole is a student here. Unbelievable! How annoying."

"It is worse than that." Jason whispered. "We still do not know what Professor Cornelius, AKA Commander Chimp, did to her."

When Jason had been held captive by the villain, Commander Chimp had boasted that he had created the perfect champion. Jason had thought he meant DeDe. But he was wrong. During Jason's captivity, Commander Chimp monologued that he had performed some sort of experimentation on Nicole. Jason wasn't sure if he was more surprised that Nicole was involved or that super villains actually monologued.

Jason leaned in closer and continued, "More importantly, we still do not know why she was chosen by him. It may not be a coincidence that she is here. She may . . ."

"Oh, it's not a coincidence; she's clearly here to torment me." DeDe slammed her locker hard, and the sonic boom echoed down the hallway.

Jason gave her a stern look. "Not too dramatic. Ix-nay on the y-sky ength-stray," he said in pig Latin.

"Seriously? You are just weird." DeDe examined her battered and dented locker and the damage she had caused. She lowered her head whispered, "Sorry. I just hate her."

Jason's stern look softened into a sympathetic one. "I know. Do not worry. Everything will be okay."

"If you tell me to 'buck up, li'l camper,' I'll slam you harder than that locker."

Jason smiled. "I cannot imagine what you would do if I said, 'stiff upper lip and all that.'" He faked an English accent, which was so horrible that it always made DeDe smile, which she did. They both laughed all the way to their first class of the day.

It was going to be an interesting year.

CHAPTER 5

Several Weeks Later

Early Monday morning, Principal Vilbran stalked down the long center hallway of the Debole Academy at a quick pace. His wing-tipped shoes clicked as he raced down the corridor. The principal carried a very small tattered notebook and a determined look. As usual, he was in a foul mood.

Although most of the world had forgotten, the principal had once been known to the world at large as the Evil Brain—deputy leader of the Retallion Battalion. He was also partner to the villainous Professor Z, the evil genius responsible for the defeat of the teen hero known as SkyBoy. Vilbran regretted that he hadn't been there to witness Professor Z's triumph, but he was sure it had been magnificent. Now he continued with their master plan.

Soon the world would be his.

Unfortunately, Vilbran's plan had met a recent complication. SkyBoy had apparently returned, and the hero's arrival could not have come at a more inopportune time. Vilbran scowled.

He had already lost the Choyut Dragon as well as Commander Chimp, his chief scientist, to the costumed avenger.

Vilbran muttered under his breath to no one in particular, "My plans have come too far to let that whelp stop me." He vowed to stop the young hero. He was sure that the tattered notebook clutched in his hand was the key. The villain had found it in the remains of the gymnasium after MechApe had self-destructed. The pages that had survived contained detailed descriptions of what could only be Sky powers. If he could find a way to decipher the rest, Vilbran knew he would have a clue about the hero's true identity.

"Oh, Principal Vilbran?" a high pitched voice called from behind him, distracting him from his obsessive thoughts and stopping him in his tracks.

The principal pivoted and turned to look down the hall at the speaker. A short, rotund man in a grey suit rushed toward Vilbran as fast as his short legs could take him.

"Hello, Superintendent August." Over the summer, August "Augie" Meadows had been chosen to serve as school superintendent. His predecessor had prematurely retired after a surprise inspection visit to the Debole Academy.

This was Augie's first visit to the school. Vilbran wondered if it would be his last.

"I'm glad I could catch you, Principal Vilbran. I have a few questions." Augie wheezed as he tried to catch his breath.

Vilbran noted that the older educator's white hair was slick with sweat. The little man sighed as he breathed.

"Will it take long?" Vilbran asked with annoyance. "I have a . . . staff meeting."

"Yes, preparation for the Welcome Carnival, I presume. I saw the rides being set up outside, and one of your students handed me this lovely flyer." Augie spoke with excitement as he took a small crumpled and colorful advertisement for the annual Debole Academy Welcome Celebration out of his pocket.

"Yes. That must be it," Vilbran replied in condescension.

Augie still gushed, oblivious to Vilbran's tone as he traced the outline of the illustration of a Ferris wheel on the handout. "I just love the Ferris wheel—going around and around without a care in the world. Around and around." He continued to trace the picture as he stared dreamily into space imagining what his journey would be like in his mind's eye.

"Superintendent August?" Vilbran asked, "Is there a reason for this visit? Or are you simply here to wax poetic about carnival rides?"

"Oh, yes." Augie returned to reality as he shoved the pamphlet back in his pocket. "I'm not sure if you know why I was chosen as superintendent."

Vilbran rolled his eyes and muttered under his breath, "Is it because you are as wide as you are tall?"

Augie didn't hear. "It was my attention to detail. For example, I was reviewing your budget reports." Vilbran watched in disgust as the superintendent fumbled with his leather satchel. Augie reached in and took a clipboard out of his briefcase. A manila folder was attached.

"My budget reports?" Vilbran stood up to his full six-foot height and glared at Augie. The principal easily towered over the four-foot, eight-inch-tall superintendent. But Augie did not notice. He was too busy rummaging through his folder.

"Ah, yes, yes. Here it is." Augie pointed to a pie chart in the folder on the clipboard. "It appears that the Debole Academy uses more than five hundred times the amount of chemicals and electronics as all of the other schools put together. And don't get me started on your electric bills . . ." Augie said as he continued to flip through a report in a manila folder, oblivious to Vilbran's glare.

"Perhaps that is why we have the best science department in the state." Vilbran snarled. Augie's predecessor's laissez-faire attitude would have never bothered with such minor details as monthly utility expense reports. In fact, the previous superintendent had never interfered in dealings at the Debole Academy for almost his entire tenure. At least he never did until that last surprise inspection. Vilbran snarled as he remembered how Shadow had remedied the situation.

Vilbran wondered how Augie would fair after staring at Orb of Anacostium and made a mental note to speak with Shadow.

Augie failed to see the grin on Vilbran's face or hear the anger in his voice as he flipped through his charts. "Ah yes, in the nearly thirteen years since you joined the Academy, you have been able to attract some rather unique and accomplished educators. But these numbers—I mean, how much power does it take to run a school?"

Vilbran took the spreadsheet and smiled at the little man's paper. "I'm sure there's an error. I will check these against my records." The two simultaneously held on to the paper and stared at each other. Vilbran added pleasantly, "As I said, I have a meeting."

"But I made a chart," Augie protested. "But . . . ."

"But"—Vilbran's lips curled into a wicked smile—"I will be glad to meet you later at the festival to discuss your numbers. Perhaps we could meet before the festival starts and I could arrange for a preview ride on the Ferris wheel."

"The Ferris wheel?" Augie asked in wonder as his eyes widened. Almost mesmerized, the superintendent let go of the folder.

"It is the largest wheel in the state," Vilbran bragged. "Our Ferris wheel also boasts completely enclosed luxury cars. If you're interested, we can set up a time later . . ." He pulled the folder further away from the superintendent.

"Five o'clock?" Augie said hopefully.

Vilbran lowered his voice and whispered like a co-conspirator. "Better make it two o'clock. We don't want you to be disturbed on your long ride."

"Very well. We wouldn't want that," Augie replied in an equally hushed whisper before he turned to leave.

Vilbran watched as Augie walked down the hall. He was sure that he noticed an added spring in the superintendent's step as the older man's shoes squeaked down the long hallway.

Finally, Augie was gone and Vilbran was alone in the corridor. Vilbran crushed the folder in his fist. "Fool," he muttered under his breath. The principal threw the spreadsheets into the nearest trash receptacle and continued his walk down the hallway.

At the dead end of the hallway, the principal stopped in front of a blank concrete wall and checked to ensure he hadn't been followed. When he was satisfied that no one was spying, Vilbran pressed a well-concealed, nearly invisible button hidden near the corner of the wall. The concrete cement shimmered a moment before the wall vanished, revealing a hidden passageway. He walked through the newly revealed door into the secret passage and entered the hidden chamber. Arcane symbols glowed on the walls and illuminated the hallway.

Halfway down the passageway to the chamber, a small three-foot-tall creature blocked Vilbran's way. He looked down at the little gnome with derision. "Gremlin, Superintendent August will be visiting the Ferris wheel this afternoon. Make sure everything is in order to ensure that the superintendent's visit is a memorable one."

The creature named Gremlin nodded enthusiastically. "Yes, master!" He remembered that he carried a hooded crimson robe and quickly offered it to Vilbran. "They have gathered for you, master. I have also brought the ceremonial garb!"

"No, Gremlin." Vilbran waved the creature away. "The time for anonymity has passed."

Vilbran stormed passed Gremlin and walked into a candlelit room at the end of the passageway. Several people of various heights and weights gathered in the room. Each one was dressed in a red, black, or white robe, concealing their identities. The gathered assembly of robed figures looked up at the sound of Vilbran's entrance. Voices murmured in concern when they saw he was not in his ceremonial garb.

Vilbran silenced the voices with a wave of his hand. "Brothers and sisters, after more than a decade, our goal is nearly at hand," he announced. "The time has come to reveal ourselves to the world."

One by one, people in the room began to whisper in anticipation. Some removed their hoods to reveal the faces of middle-aged men and women. In addition, there were some exotic-looking creatures. One had green scales, another had blue fur, and a third was covered with yellow feathers. Still other occupants' appearances were so hideous that they continued to hide their faces under their hoods for fear of causing a riot. A menacing figure moved into the shadows in the corner of the room and blended with them.

Gremlin became agitated as he squealed, "Tell us, tell us, tell us your plan, oh magnificent master." The gnome screamed with glee as he jumped up and down in the small chamber.

Vilbran tried to ignore the hopping creature and looked upon the hopeful faces of his followers. "The convergence is upon us once again. We must begin the final phase. We will gather what we need. Victory will be ours."

"Wonderful." One of the men exhaled in dramatic fashion. "More delusions of grandeur."

Several people shuffled away from the speaker, creating a pathway between him and Vilbran.

The speaker wore horn-rimmed glasses and had a boyish face. He held a magic eight ball in his hand.

Vilbran recognized the man. "Ah, Professor Nicholas Nack — or do you prefer your *nom de guerre*, Nicknack?" Vilbran immediately moved to intercept the evil inventor. "Do I sense sarcasm?"

Nicknack removed his glasses and cleaned them. "Not sarcasm—realism. For years we have patiently waited for your great plan to be fulfilled. Now we are supposed to believe that you're ready. I find it very suspicious that this great revelation comes so closely after the return of . . . "

"Don't say that name!" Vilbran shrieked. "Do not sully this sacred hall of evil with even the mention of that do-gooder's name."

"Touched a nerve?" Nicknack asked proudly as he replaced his glasses and shook his eight ball. "Perhaps your former partner was not as successful as we were led to believe."

Nicknack placed an unusually strong emphasis on the word partner.

Vilbran ignored the insinuation and calmed himself. "He is not back. It is someone else with similar powers. I have his notebook, and soon I will have his identity. Although this boy has the powers, he lacks experience and will not present a problem. We will move forward with our plan, gather the energy, and then. . ."

"And then what?" Nicknack interrupted. He shook the eight ball more furiously. "You have lost the chimp. You don't have the Choyut Dragon. Without that, you cannot focus the energy necessary to—"

"We will get it back," Vilbran said calmly as he walked to a podium in the front of the room. It was then that Vilbran noticed some of the other occupants nodding in agreement with Nicknack. This type of dissension simply would not do. Vilbran reached under the podium and removed a large black helmet. He placed the headpiece over his head until it covered his entire face.

Nicknack ignored Vilbran and held up the magic eight ball. He dramatically shook the plastic ball and asked, "Will Evil Brain's ridiculous plan succeed?" With equal flair, Nicknack turned over the black ball. "Signs point to no."

Some people in the room chuckled. Others soon joined. Suddenly, the sound of uncomfortable laughter was drowned out by the sound of an electrical charge as an energy bolt shot from Evil Brain's helmet. The beam shot across the room and struck Nicknack in the chest. The inventor didn't even have time to scream before he disintegrated into a smoldering pile of white powder on the cold chamber floor.

Evil Brain stared down at the crowd. "I believe Nicknack has made his opinion and dissension known. Does anyone else have any other concerns I can address?" The helmet made Vilbran's baritone voice reverberate and sound deeper, mechanical, and more menacing.

"Uh, Mr. Evil Brain, sir?" a woman asked in an English accent. Evil Brain immediately recognized the voice of Beatrice Tick, the school librarian.

"Yes, Beatrice?" Evil Brain asked in an annoyed tone.

"Um, what should we do about Sky—" His glare caused her to correct herself. "This. . . um . . . insignificant but powerful boy?" She braced for the lightning.

"Nothing. I will handle it when the time is right," Evil Brain commanded as he removed his helmet. "But now Gremlin and I must go and prepare for my meeting with Superintendent August." He looked at the powder stain on the floor. "Find someone to take over Professor Nack's shop class."

"But the boy—" someone started to ask.

"Will be dealt with," Vilbran interrupted. As an afterthought, he turned back to the assembled masses. "But we must be vigilant. This individual has defeated Commander Chimp and his Gorilla Army. This insolent whelp may be inexperienced, but he is also smart, sharp, and will not be carelessly caught. At this very moment, this hero is focused on one thing: using his powers to stop us. This individual is single minded. We must be the same."

Vilbran turned and stormed out of the room.

CHAPTER 6

At that moment, the single-minded individual Evil Brain had referred to was focused on one thing. "Do you think the purple cape and skirt make my hips look fat?" DeDe asked as she leaned back in her seat and stared dreamily at the ceiling.

"Will you focus on the math homework?" Jason chided.

"Math is hard."

"Duly noted, you sound like that Barbie doll you had when you were little. What did you get for number two?" Jason asked.

"I mean, the spandex is slimming, but the purple is so . . . Maybe if I added a bigger belt," DeDe mused.

Jason was fighting a losing battle. He closed his math book and threw it in his backpack, removing a small notebook from his open bag. "Your belt is fine. But as long as we are on the SG subject..." He lowered his voice to a whisper. "I never asked you; How was the domino?"

DeDe gave him a curious look. "What question was that?"

"The domino. You know, the little mask you wore when you faced the Gorilla Army."

"Oh." She grinned as she realized the costume conversation had trumped the discussion over math homework. "It was okay. I liked it better than that other one. At least I could see." DeDe spoke in a loud mock whisper and then chuckled. Jason looked around and realized that they were the only ones in the classroom; he felt silly for whispering and blushed.

DeDe smiled with pride. She loved giving her best friend a hard time.

He made a notation in the book. "That is great about the mask."

Over the summer, Jason and DeDe had experimented with several different ways to disguise her identity. First, Jason had her wear a purple wig. During their test runs there were lots of problems. First it kept flying off at high speed, and then, after they pinned it down, it burst into flames at SkySpeed. Jason concluded that the aura that surrounded DeDe and protected her Sky Girl costume only worked on skintight fabric and would not extend to a wig. DeDe was not happy with the experience. He wondered if she had forgotten about it yet.

"It's a lot better than that stupid purple wig," DeDe mused as if reading Jason's mind. She glared at him. "You know, I'm still picking melted nylon out of my hair."

"For the umpteenth time, I'm sorry," Jason apologized. He looked at his notes. After the wig fiasco, they had tried a traditional mask. Unfortunately, DeDe's peripheral vision had been blocked and her depth perception was off. As a result, she kept flying into walls, doors, and the ground. It made quite a mess and Jason spent the majority of the income from his summer job at the hardware store buying plaster and spackle.

On the night of her battle with Commander Chimp's Gorilla Army, they had tried a small purple mask, which was set in

40

place with a special dissolving spirit gum created by the galactic Protectorate.

"The domino is a success, then. Now Sky Girl has a mask," he said with finality. "And your secret identity is safe."

DeDe reached into her bag, pulled out the purple mask, and held it up to her face. "I don't know. Don't you think it's a little small? I mean, you can still see my face."

Jason took his friend by the hand. "DeDe, you are my best friend, and I am always honest with you. But sometimes you are clueless. Do you really believe that when someone sees a young, hot, athletic girl in tight spandex, they are going to be focused on her face?"

DeDe blushed and pulled her hand back. She put the mask into her bag and stood up. She looked in the mirror by the classroom door and struck a pose like a body builder. Over the summer, DeDe's powers had begun to affect her physical appearance. She hadn't gotten any taller, but she was no longer a scrawny little girl. She had developed washboard abs and defined muscles. At Jason's insistence, DeDe had started to wear baggy clothes so no one could see the nearly overnight change. DeDe turned to Jason, put her hand to her face, and spoke in a fake airhead voice, "So you really think I'm hot? OMG! I can't wait to write it in my diary."

Jason blushed. "Um, I... Um."

DeDe's voice returned to a normal, stern tone. "Somehow I think that was supposed to be a compliment, right? Not too awkward. Uncool, man."

Jason blushed a deeper crimson as he nodded. "Sorry."

"Forget it." Satisfied with the result, DeDe changed the subject. "We'd better get to three o'clock shop class."

41

Jason welcomed the conversation change and picked up his backpack. "Mister Nack will give us detention if we are late again." As if to punctuate his statement, a bell rang. "Race you."

"Let's go then. What are you waiting for?" DeDe said with a smile as she rushed to the door at SkySpeed.

Jason rolled his eyes and followed. "That is cheating!"

In order to save time, they cut across the football field, which had been converted into a makeshift festival fairground. Jason stared at all the rides and games. A large black Ferris wheel towered over the rest of the attractions. "Wow. I do not remember the Ferris wheel looking so . . . sinister."

DeDe grabbed his arm and yanked. "Focus! We can't be late again."

Minutes later, they rushed into the classroom for their final class, beating the second bell by a mere second.

"I can't believe we made it." Jason exhaled slowly as he tried to catch his breath.

"Wow." DeDe gestured to the front of the room. "We even beat Mr. Nack."

Jason took his seat. "I ran..for...nothing," he huffed.

DeDe tried not to laugh at her out-of-shape friend. She failed.

Jason grumbled as he glared at her. Before he could say another word, the door opened and Beatrice Tick, the school librarian, walked in.

"Mr. Nack is . . . ah . . . indisposed. I will be covering his class, today," she announced.

"Miss Tick?" Kaycee Saiz asked as she raised her hand. "When will Mr. Nack be back? "

Jason looked at DeDe and rubbed his nose. DeDe suppressed a giggle.

"Um," the school librarian responded, "I'm not sure he will be able to pull himself together anytime soon. Until then, this is a free period." The librarian appeared overly proud with her response and somewhat amused by her cleverness.

"A free period! Great, we can finish the math homework," Jason sang as he opened his backpack.

"Yeah, that's great, just super." DeDe's words dripped with sarcasm.

Jason looked nervous.

"What's wrong?" she asked.

"My math notebook is gone. It was in here." Jason dumped the contents of his bag on the desk. "It is gone."

"I don't have it," DeDe confirmed as she looked in her backpack.

Jason turned pale. "It is gone and lost forever. I am going to fail."

"Wow. I thought I was a drama queen." DeDe rolled her eyes.

Jason took a moment from his tantrum and looked up at her. "You are a drama queen, but that does not change the fact that I lost my notebook."

DeDe smiled. "Calm down. Let's just retrace your steps."

"Okay." Jason cast his eyes toward the ceiling and tried to remember. "We were across campus talking about S—" Jason saw Ms. Tick looking at him then and censored himself. "— talking about stuff. Then we cut across . . ." Jason slapped his head. "Of course. I must have dropped it at the fairgrounds near the Ferris wheel. I'd better go look for it."

DeDe put her hand on his shoulder and spoke in a sincere tone. "I'll go. I can cover more ground. You finish the rest of the homework." She went to Miss Tick and returned with a hall pass, grabbing her backpack as she whispered in Jason's ear, "In case I need a better sky eye's view to find it. Besides, we both know that my eyesight is better since you lost your contacts." DeDe winked and skipped out of the room.

Jason was relieved. He could do the rest of the problems while DeDe retrieved the first half.

A second later, he realized that his best friend had just tricked him into doing all the math homework.

CHAPTER 7

DeDe smiled as she skipped down the hallway with her backpack slung over her shoulder. Although it wasn't fair to Jason, DeDe was still quite pleased with herself. She'd gotten out of class and her math homework. Her plan was to quickly run out to the fairground and get Jason's math notebook. It shouldn't take long.

Maybe, afterward, she could also "accidentally" run into Adam after his Physics class.

At that moment, down at the fairgrounds, Superintendent August stood on the football field. He checked his watch again, noting that it was a quarter after two. Principal Vilbran was late. Fearing he had been stood up, the superintendent turned and was about to head up to the school. Before he could leave, however, he looked up at the large carnival rides and became fixed in place.

A large Ferris wheel stood in the center of the fairground. The words *Wheel of Fortune* were emblazoned in multicolored neon lights on the side of the ride.

"Do you like it?" Vilbran called from the shadows.

August jumped at the noise. "I didn't see you there," he gasped, embarrassed, but his thoughts turned to other things as he looked up at the Ferris wheel again. "It is very impressive," he gushed.

"It was designed by Professor Cornelius, a former teacher and associate," Vilbran said with pride. "Sadly, he is no longer working here at the Debole Academy."

"Did he switch schools?" August asked.

Vilbran ignored his question. "Would you like a ride?"

"Oh, I couldn't. Still, it is impressive. I assume it is safe?" August asked, debating with himself.

Vilbran sneered. "I assure you that it will perform exactly the way it was intended and do precisely what it was designed to do."

"Excellent." August pranced over to the machine. "Then I would be remiss in my duties if I let students go on this ride before I tested it. Let's go for a ride—you know, for safety's sake, I mean."

"For safety's sake, of course." Vilbran repeated as he opened the large door on the side of the Ferris wheel car. "You go and I will operate the machinery."

August ducked his head down and entered the car. "Oh yes, Augie my boy, this is going to be a most exciting ride." The superintendent cooed to himself.

"You have no idea." Vilbran muttered as he slammed the door. Vilbran could hear as Superintendent August clicked the seatbelt. The principal removed a small black remote control from his pocket and pressed a green button. The Ferris wheel hummed to life.

August cheered as the ride began to move.

Vilbran allowed Augie to enjoy the ride for a few moments before he pressed the red button on the controller. "Goodbye, superintendent," he said with a sneer as he turned to walk back into the school.

As he entered a darkened alcove that led back up to the building, Vilbran glanced at his watch. He still had a few minutes before his next meeting, so he turned back to watch Augie's demise. For all his recent administrative duties, Vilbran still enjoyed getting his hands dirty now and then.

The Ferris wheel spun faster and faster. Vilbran watched as it became a blur on the field. He listened as Augie's squeals of delight turned into screams of pain, and a small grin formed on the principal's face.

"Help! Help!" August screamed as the machine spun faster and faster. Suddenly, the car jerked and the superintendent's head slammed back against the metal backing of the car. He slumped into a semi-conscious haze.

The principal stared at the Ferris wheel with interest. This was one of Cornelius' better creations. It would not be long until the superintendent was crushed by the centrifugal force. Vilbran frowned. It would be over too quickly. The principal had not even had to the opportunity to test Cornelius' other enhancements to the deadly attraction.

Suddenly, Vilbran saw a purple and black blur streak across the sky toward the Ferris wheel. The sight immediately piqued the principal's interest. He watched as the blur approached his amusement park death trap. In the distance, he watched a figure wearing what could only be a purple cape place both hands on the side of the Ferris wheel car and yank on the ride. There was a loud grinding noise as the car ripped from its casings.

The sudden force at which the car ripped free caused August's head to slam hard again against the back of the ride. The superintendent groaned in pain and slumped down.

"Oops, sorry," the figure muttered in a high-pitched voice.

Vilbran hid in the shadows and watched as this new SkyBoy pretender saved the superintendent. He peered at the costumed individual and corrected himself. It was not a boy at all. This was a girl—a Sky Girl. He removed the remote from his pocket. "Well, 'Sky Girl,' I guess it is time we tested the limits of your abilities by seeing what Professor Cornelius' machine is capable of doing."

Across the field, Sky Girl slowly carried the Ferris wheel car down to the grassy earth of the fairgrounds.

"Hold on," Sky Girl instructed as she gently placed the Ferris wheel car on the ground. "I'll have you out in a sec." Once the ride vehicle was safely on the ground, Sky Girl ripped the door off the hinges with one hand and continued to hold it above her head. With her free hand, Sky Girl helped the superintendent out of the car. "You'll be okay now," she said in a deep voice, attempting to sound reassuring. "So, um, what happened?"

"Oh, my head." August groaned. He looked at the costumed teenager standing in front of him, holding the heavy metal door. "Oh, dear. I must have hit my head harder than I thought." He rubbed his head.

"What happened?" Sky Girl repeated, trying not to smile at the odd little man.

Before August could answer, he fainted on the grass. Sky Girl moved to help the collapsed superintendent.

But before Sky Girl could reach August, a loud grinding noise emitted once again from the Ferris wheel. The costumed heroine turned to see the ride move under its own power. It wasn't just moving; it was transforming from a carnival attraction into something else. The center of the ride collapsed, and the cars connected on four sides, forming arms and legs. The middle of the wheel stretched until it looked like a large ape-like skull, which glared menacingly at the teenage girl and the elderly superintendent. Then, with a loud growl, the Ferris wheel completed its transformation into a menacing, giant robot ape.

Sky Girl knew that Jason would have loved to have seen this transformation. She also knew that she had seen this robotic creature before.

"MechApe!" Sky Girl said the name like a curse under her breath. In her first outing as Sky Girl, she had faced the menace of MechApe, or rather a different version of the creature. The original MechApe had self-destructed and was responsible for the demolition of the gymnasium.

Realizing that she was still holding the Ferris wheel door, Sky Girl threw the large metal door at the creature. Without hesitation, the young heroine launched from the ground and flew at full speed toward the creature's chest plate. The creature easily batted away the door but did not expect the two-pronged attack as Sky Girl flew toward the monster at SkySpeed. A second before impact, she punched the creature with all her might. The impact echoed off the buildings like a sonic boom.

Sky Girl floated in the air next to MechApe and assessed the damage she had inflicted. She pouted. Other than a small dent in the creature's chest plate, MechApe was otherwise undamaged.

Just then, MechApe turned its red eyes and look directly at her.

"That's not good," she uttered before the creature nonchalantly swatted Sky Girl away. The metallic fist collided with her in a loud slam. The force of the impact knocked Sky Girl across the fairgrounds. She crashed into a table and chairs set up at the festival kissing booth, which splintered with the impact and knocked the wind out of the costumed heroine.

Sky Girl slowly stood up and looked sadly at the remains. Adam had signed up to work at that booth.

Sky Girl looked up at MechApe and then stared off into the distance.

The creature roared a challenge at the girl, causing the hairs on the back of her neck to rise.

A second later, Sky Girl took to the sky and flew away from the scene at SkySpeed.

MechApe watched her retreat. The monster roared triumphantly and banged its large arms on its chest.

Vilbran watched the scene with disgust. He had expected a challenge. This new heroine was nothing. One hit and she ran away like a spoiled little child. He turned to re-enter the school and report his findings to the Retallion Battalion. At least Commander Chimp's last invention had been a success.

Suddenly, Vilbran heard a loud noise that sounded like howling wind. He turned back from the door and looked up into the sky to see what could be making such noise. The afternoon sun blazed near the horizon. He squinted into the bright light and saw a large object flying toward the fair grounds. Vilbran wondered if it was an airplane or a helicopter.

No, it was not an aircraft at all. It was a teenage girl dressed in black and purple. She carried a large cylindrical object. Although the barrel-shaped object was more than ten times her size, she carried it with ease.

"Hey, MechApe!" Sky Girl taunted as she threw the object at the confused mechanical monkey. "Surf's up!"

MechApe moved to block the projectile.

"Clever girl." Vilbran sighed. He had calculated the heroine's strategy a second before the water tower crashed into the robot. The contents of the tower splashed against the creatures exposed wires and shorted them out. The drenched mechanical monkey began to spark. It was a variation on what had happened to the creature's predecessor in the gymnasium pool.

Vilbran watched as Sky Girl stared at the creature. Given the similarities of her other powers to SkyBoy's, he surmised that she also must possess some sort of SkyVision. The teen held up her hands and shot a concentrated burst of energy into the creature's chest. "Of course. A Skypulse," Vilbran muttered.

The creature tumbled to the ground, the red lights in its eyes fading to darkness.

Vilbran frowned and tried to take solace in the fact that MechApe's self-destruct mechanism would soon be activated. In a moment, the explosion would destroy both the fairgrounds and the heroine. The sacrifice would be worth it. He could easily rebuild the fairgrounds. The girl would not be as lucky.

Across the field, Sky Girl giggled and said, "Our relationship is getting too serious, ape face. I think you need some space . . outer space."

Almost faster than the Vilbran's eyes could process, Sky Girl moved under the creature. The young heroine grabbed one of MechApe's bulky arms and whipped the creature around her in a circular motion. She leaned back as she spun the creature faster and faster, resembling an Olympic athlete in the hammer throw.

"Clever girl," Vilbran repeated as Sky Girl finally let go of the creature. The monster flew into the sky.

Moments later, MechApe exploded several hundred feet above the fairgrounds. Debris rained down on the fairgrounds.

Sky Girl rushed over to the fallen superintendent. She brushed a strand of red hair from her face and examined him. With ease, she picked up the overweight man like a rag doll and began to float into the sky.

Vilbran watched with interest as something made the girl stop. She slowly floated down to the ground and started toward his hiding place.

Vilbran held his breath as the heroine approached. If she discovered him, all would be lost. He wasn't ready to deal with this upstart yet. He began to panic.

Sky Girl moved to a position three feet away from the alcove and stopped. Balancing the superintendent over her shoulder, Sky Girl carefully bent down and scooped up a small three-subject notebook. With a satisfied smile, she flew into the sky with a blur.

Sky Girl was gone.

Vilbran slowly exhaled, then cursed himself for his momentary fear. Vilbran reassessed the situation as he rushed back into the school. Clearly, his Retallion Battalion could beat a little girl. Things had certainly changed. He needed to find out more about this Sky Girl.

Later that night, DeDe and Jason sat in the basement of 16 Hartland Court. DeDe had just finished acting out her battle in the fairgrounds.

Jason pouted. "I cannot believe I missed a transforming MechApe."

"You didn't miss anything. It was over pretty quickly. I'm glad we practiced that spinny thing. I can't imagine what would have happened if he went all self-destructy on the ground."

"Discus Maneuver seven," Jason corrected indignantly.

"I'm sorry. I meant Dorkus Maneuver Seven," DeDe teased before adding, with a more serious tone, "You think Chimp-Face is back?"

"I am not sure. I have to assume that Coach Lee would have found some way to warn us." He added under his breath, "If she could."

DeDe thought about her old coach, Sam "Samantha" Hung Lee, guardian of the Choyut dragon. Commander Chimp had turned her entire village into half-human, half-tiger hybrids. During the Nationals, Coach Lee, in tiger form, had saved Jason from Commander Chimp while DeDe had fought the first MechApe. After the fight, Coach Lee had vanished, taking both the Choyut dragon and the chimpanzee villain with her. But before she disappeared, she left a secret message that explained that she had known the original SkyBoy and that he would have been proud of her: the new Sky Girl.

DeDe's eyes began to tear up. She realized that Jason was staring at her. "What? I miss her, okay?"

"I was saying that I think this may be something new," Jason said, trying to keep on point.

"Great! Just what we need." DeDe pouted as she copied Jason's math homework.

Then she looked up with a smile. "Do you think it's our math teacher?"

CHAPTER 8

One Week Later

The sun rose on a Saturday morning and illuminated the exterior of 16 Hartland Court, making the normally white exterior of the building appear burnt orange. Inside the house, Jason and DeDe took part in their weekly ritual: Saturday Morning Movie Madness. Neither could remember how the tradition began or who had started it, but for the past ten years, DeDe and Jason took turns picking out movies. The pair would then sit on DeDe's purple coach in the basement and stare at the small 16-inch television that sat on a metal TV stand. It started with cartoons, but as DeDe and Jason grew older, their movie tastes expanded.

Unfortunately for DeDe, it was Jason's turn to pick the movie.

The small television displayed a black-and-white picture of panicked townspeople as they rushed through a shopping mall. A second later, a horde of disfigured zombies followed them through the mall. The creatures uttered monosyllabic grunts and groans as they passed juice bars and electronics stores in their attempts to catch the townspeople. Enraptured, Jason leaned forward and stared at the images on the screen. The light flickered off his wrinkled jeans and white *Honk if you are about to hit me!* T-shirt.

He sighed in admiration and turned to his best friend. "You see, DeDe, the whole movie is a metaphor for society. That is why they end up in a shopping mall and the hardware store. I cannot believe how much of a genius Romero is."

DeDe sighed louder. "And I can't believe you're making me watch zombies on Saturday Morning Movie Madness . . ." She paused for dramatic effect before adding, "Again." DeDe wore her faded blue jeans and an oversized purple sweatshirt with the words "Dance" printed on it in pink. Her red hair was put up in a ponytail, which made her look younger.

"I like zombies," Jason protested.

"We could've at least watched one of my vampire movies."

"No, we could not. Your vampire movies are ridiculous, and the characters arguably do not even qualify as vampires."

"Oh yeah? They have vampire powers."

Jason sighed as he turned to her. "How many times do I have to explain this? Throughout history and folklore, vampires have been the most powerful creatures in the universe. But in your movies, the only power vampires possess is the ability to look hot and the willpower to stand by their troubled girlfriends."

DeDe huffed.

Jason added, "What? Would it help if I said that I am on team Sky Girl."

DeDe laughed and tried to suggest a different movie. "We could get—"

"Hey, it was my turn to pick. How many times have you made me sit through *White Knights?* We are not watching it."

"How did you know I was going to suggest *White Knights?*"

Jason rolled his eyes again. "You always suggest *White Knights.*"

DeDe leaned forward in excitement. "It's a classic. You know I have a copy of it around. We could—"

Jason turned back to the set. "Good. Then we can watch that when it is your turn."

DeDe pouted. "But it's—"

"My turn," he interrupted.

Sensing defeat, DeDe turned to logic. "You know, *White Knights* is a great movie, and I can use it to learn some new moves for...you know." She made flying motion with her hand.

Jason ignored her, and DeDe flopped back on the couch in defeat. "Your zombie movies are just dumb."

"Actually, a good zombie movie has very little to do with zombies. It is really about the survivors and how they deal in the aftermath of a zombie attack. Robert Kirkman said—"

"Well then, I stand corrected." DeDe brushed a strand of hair from her face and mimicked Jason's tone. "Actually, your movies about survivors and how they deal in the aftermath of a zombie attack are stupid."

"You know, this could also be helpful in case Sky Girl ever . . ." He trailed off.

DeDe giggled. "In case Sky Girl ever . . ."

Jason avoided her gaze. "You know."

DeDe poked him in the ribs. "In case I ever what? Face a zombie horde in a hardware store?"

Jason tried not laugh at the tickle. "It could happen."

"There's more of a chance of being trapped behind the iron curtain with Baryshnikov." She thought about it for a moment and swooned. "That wouldn't be half bad. Michal and I facing incredible odds with only our dancing to . . ."

"Shh," Jason said. "This is my favorite part."

The small screen showed a vacant lot, and the camera slowly panned the ground.

Jason leaned in closer.

DeDe picked up a dance magazine. "You said the same thing about the last five scenes."

Jason shushed her again.

The sound of footsteps emitted from the small speaker as Jason moved so close to the set, his nose nearly touched the screen.

DeDe groaned. "Please. You own this movie. You know what's going to happen."

"Shhh!"

A large, lizard-like alien face filled the screen. The sudden appearance of the creature startled Jason, who fell back from the set and then off the couch. "Uh, DeDe!"

DeDe did not look up from her magazine. "For goodness' sake, now you're just being a drama queen."

"DeDe."

DeDe continued, "I mean, how many times have you seen this movie? There is no way you—"

"DeDe!" yelled Jason.

The lizard spoke in a soft but assertive voice. "Deirdre Christopher, Sky Girl is needed."

Discarding her magazine, DeDe jumped up and rushed to the television set. "Boosadah? On my TV?"

Jason got up from the floor and tried to press the wrinkles out of his jeans and shirt as he stood in front of the television. "Boosadah?" He looked closer and recognized a living version of the alien from his comic books.

She closed her eyes and nodded in affirmation.

Jason moved closer to the set. "Your Excellency, this is an honor. I cannot believe that you would come here and... Wow. It must be very important for you to appear on the television set from the Protectorate. The power it takes to accomplish this must be incredible. This must be something big, like that time in issue two-ninety-two of Daringly Fresh Adventures of—"

DeDe sighed. "If you would stop rambling, maybe she'll tell us."

Jason sat down on the couch. "I am not rambling. I am analyzing. Admittedly, I am a little excited at the prospect of alien first contact. Well, obviously not first, but . . ."

DeDe smiled. "Whatevs."

Jason huffed as he crossed his arms over his chest and sat on the couch. "Whatevs, indeed."

The alien's image ignored Jason and turned to DeDe. "Dierdre, there is a problem in the Mutardi Dimension. One of our operatives needs Sky Girl's help."

"Mutardi?" Jason pondered. "Is Colonel Kirby in trouble?"

The black-and-white visage of Boosadah shimmered. "How did you . . ."

Jason leaned back and put his hands behind his head. "You will find I am full of surprises."

"He's certainly full of something." DeDe gave Jason a mischievous grin and a shove, which knocked him off the couch.

Boosadah yawned. "Ah, this must be the witty banter I have heard so much about. Colonel Kirby was on an important mission. He has not checked in and may be in trouble, child. You must fly out to the Mutardi Dimension and assist him with his mission if you can."

DeDe's mouth dropped open in shock. "Dimension? You want me to fly into outer space?"

Boosadah and Jason spoke at the same time. "Not exactly outer space."

DeDe put her hands to her head. "Not exactly outer space. Where—"

Boosadah and Jason spoke in unison again. "Pocket space."

DeDe rolled her eyes. "Great—stereogeek."

Boosadah and Jason glared at DeDe.

"Sorry. Go ahead."

Boosadah grimaced. "Mr. Shewstal, if you are so knowledgeable, perhaps you want to explain?"

Jason shook his head. "No. No, you can do it. It is your Protectorate, after all."

Boosadah's face became calm. "The Mutardi Dimension exists in a pocket dimension, just outside normal space. It is not outer space, but outside of space."

"Whatevs." DeDe brushed the strand of hair that fell into her face. "Just give me a map. I'll find it."

Jason stood. "When do we leave?"

"There is no *we*, Mr. Shewstal. Deirdre must go alone."

"Listen, I am not sure if you are aware, but DeDe and I have handled a lot of missions together," Jason said indignantly.

"Mr. Shewstal."

"I know a lot," he continued.

"Boosadah, it sounds like this is serious," DeDe said in defense of her friend. "I may need some help, and Jason—"

"Cannot breathe in the Mutardi Dimension. It is toxic to humans." Boosadah sighed.

DeDe stared at the screen in disbelief, and Jason threw up his hands and turned away from the set.

"Well, then. I guess that settles it. DeDe goes to the toxic dimension. I will wait in the car."

DeDe stared at the screen. "Toxic? Like the opposite of a crayon? What about me? What am I going to do?"

Boosadah sighed again. "I assumed you knew. Because of your powers, you do not need to breathe anymore." After a second she added, "Or eat or drink or sleep."

Jason whipped his notebook out from his back pocket and began to write furiously. "Complete self-sustaining cellular structure—fascinating."

DeDe slapped the book from Jason's hands. "It's not fascinating! Put that away. What do you mean I don't have to breathe anymore?"

Just then, Dianne entered the basement. "Hey, guys. Sorry to interrupt the movie, but I need a favor."

Jason and DeDe jumped at the interruption.

"Mom!" DeDe screeched.

Jason stared down at the floor.

Dianne smiled. "I wasn't interrupting anything, was I?"

Another strand of red hair fell in DeDe face as she reacted to the words. "What? No. We were just . . ." DeDe peered at the image of Boosadah on the screen.

"We were just watching this cool new retro zombie movie: Lizard Aliens versus the Zombies of Xanadu," said Jason. "I guess we really got into it."

61

Dianne looked at the screen. As if on cue, Boosadah said, "You zombie fiend! I will use my lizard ray to defeat your undead villainy."

Dianne shrugged. "I don't know how you can watch this kind of stuff. That alien looks so fake, and the acting is horrible."

Boosadah glared at Dianne.

DeDe stepped in front of her mother, blocking her view of the television set. "You said you needed something, Mom. What is it?"

Dianne handed her daughter a deposit envelope. "I got another of your father's royalty checks in today's mail. Can you go down to the First Bank of Colonia and deposit it? Michael and I are going to see Nana at the home today, and I just don't have time to go."

DeDe snatched the envelope. "Sure thing, Mom." She put it on the coffee table. "But can we finish our movie first?"

Dianne hugged her daughter. "Such responsibility."

Jason chuckled. "With great power . . ."

DeDe glared at Jason over her mother's shoulder, and Boosadah threw Jason a stern look.

Dianne walked over to the steps that led out of the basement and turned back. "Enjoy your movie. You kids behave. Don't do anything I wouldn't do."

"Mom!" DeDe shrieked.

"I wonder what she meant by that," said Jason.

DeDe blushed. "I have no idea."

When the embarrassment passed, she leaned close to the television set "What do you mean I no longer have to breathe?" she asked sternly, stressing every word in the question.

"Or sleep or eat or drink." Jason added helpfully.

DeDe was not amused.

Boosadah waved a dismissive hand. "It's all very complicated, and we do not have time. You must get to the Mutardi Dimension. The nearest entryway is a lighthouse in Menlo Park."

Jason looked up from his notebook. "You mean the Edison Memorial Tower?"

"Professor Edison was a valued advisor to the Protectorate," Boosadah continued without looking at Jason. "The dimension can be accessed through the telephone booth on the south side of the lighthouse. Dial 353-7872 to access the dimension."

Jason wrote the number in his notebook; there was something familiar about it.

"Report in when you get there." The image blinked out and was replaced by a hideous zombie.

DeDe quickly stood up. "Well, then, I guess we can't finish the movie."

Jason tore the page with the number from his notebook. "I can feel your disappointment from here." He reached over and picked up DeDe's purple backpack.

"Yep, I'm crushed."

He tossed her the pack. "I guess it is Sky time."

DeDe caught the bag and glared at her best friend. "Sky time? Seriously?"

Jason shrugged. "What? You do not like your new catch phrase? Every superhero needs one."

DeDe opened the bag and pulled her costume out of the hidden compartment in the bottom of the bag. "Well, throw that one back and catch a better one. Now turn around. I need to get dressed."

Jason pouted as he turned his back to DeDe. "I thought that was a good one. I worked hard on it." He felt his hair move in the breeze as DeDe dressed at SkySpeed.

A second later, DeDe was dressed as Sky Girl. She adjusted her purple mask in the mirror. "Try harder."

Jason turned back to Sky Girl with a frown. "Fine. You come up with one." He helped her center her cape and handed her the paper.

Sky Girl gave her friend a sympathetic hug. "We'll work on a better one when I get back tonight."

"I guess. All righty, then. Go to the Mutardi Dimension and save the world. Remember to play nice and make friends."

Another breeze blew Jason's hair, and she was gone.

He looked at the deposit envelope Dianne had placed on the coffee table. "I guess I will be waiting in line at the very dull and boring First Bank of Colonia while you are traveling through the very exciting pocket space."

He sat down and turned up the sound on the television. "After I finish the movie, of course."

CHAPTER 9

The Edison Memorial Tower and Museum, built in the 1930s, looms over the nearby residential neighborhoods. Atop the memorial sits a large replica of the first incandescent light bulb created by the inventor known as the Wizard of Menlo Park. On a clear night, the 175-foot-tall structure can be seen in several neighboring counties and from passengers on Amtrak and New Jersey Transit trains that ride on the North East Corridor line.

Sky Girl floated to the ground in front of the memorial and moved into a nearby covered alcove. The shadows helped hide her dark purple and black costume. The heroine looked up at the light bulb on the top of the building. She remembered sitting in the back of her parents' car as a child on the way home from the Menlo Park Mall. Her family would play a game to see who could catch a glimpse of the lighthouse first. She would stare at the memorial through the trees, amazed by its bulbous appearance. DeDe remembered when she and Jason had come to the lighthouse once on a field trip in middle school and visited the museum on the first floor. During that trip, DeDe learned that Thomas Edison, the inventor of the light bulb, the phonograph, and a bunch of other things, had grown up in the town next to them. She wondered if she would be remembered for anything.

"Hey there. The museum is closed on Saturday," a voice boomed out, distracting Sky Girl from her thoughts. A spotlight landed on the heroine and illuminated her black and purple costume.

"What are you doing here?" the voice asked more harshly.

Sky Girl smiled. "Um, hi." She looked down at her purple skirt. "You are probably wondering why I'm here wearing . . ."

A security guard rolled out of the shadows on a Segway. He was portly and looked to be around nineteen. A name badge on his rent-a-cop uniform labeled him as Alexander. "Listen, kid, the middle school costume party isn't until next week." Without the microphone, Alexander's voice sounded much more nasal and much less intimidating.

The costumed girl became indignant. "Middle school? Do I look like I go to—" Sky Girl stopped, smiled, and made her voice sound flightier. "Oh, darn it. I knew Mommy should have written down the date. Is there, like, a pay phone around here so I can call my mommy and daddy and have them come and pick me up?"

The guard shined his light on the side of the building, which DeDe thought was silly since it was daylight out. "Sure. There's one over there, on the south side. I'm gonna finish my rounds. Just don't be here when I get back."

"Thanks, mister. I won't." Sky Girl waited for Alexander's Segway to disappear around the building before she entered the phone booth. She took out a slip of paper and dialed the number Boosadah had given her.

66

A second later, Sky Girl disappeared in a flash of light.

On the other side of the building, Officer Alexander saw the bright flash behind him. He turned to see what had caused it without stopping his Segway and failing to see the large boulder in the grass in front of him. The Segway crashed with a loud thud, and Alexander tumbled to the ground and into the mud. With a groan, the watchman pulled himself out of the muck. "What'd I hit?" he asked as he groped for his flashlight on the ground. Finally, he found it and shined the beam in the direction of his Segway. The sun shone brightly on the landscape. When he saw the boulder that had caused his tumble, Alexander blushed and put the flashlight away. Then, he saw what was behind the rock.

"Amazing!" Alexander gasped at the large structure that had appeared out of thin air in the path in front of him. He had been working as a security guard at the museum for months but had never seen this building. The portly watchman got to his feet and approached a large metal door on the front of the structure. He walked up to and then around it; however, once he took a step past the door, it vanished before his eyes.

"Wha—?" Alexander took another step back, and the door reappeared. "Well, I'll be," Alexander mused as he ran his hand over the futuristic door.

The door chimed, "Professor Z genetic template recognized," and then swung open.

Alexander stood in surprise for a moment, then walked inside and looked around. He was in some sort of high-tech facility. Futuristic devices lined the walls of the hidden laboratory. Gray metallic flooring stretched in every direction and led to hallways that extended as far as his eyes could see.

He stared down one of the hallways. "Wow, this place is a lot bigger on the inside." His voice echoed down the hallway.

Suddenly, a long cylindrical arm emerged from a hidden panel in the ceiling. A small computer eye attached to the end of the arm blinked as it examined Alexander, and the startled watchman jumped back from it.

"Welcome," said a computer voice. "Request voice template analysis."

"Um," said Alexander.

The computer repeated a recording of Alexander's word and continued. "Voice template set. Villainous arsenal is armed and available. Please state the nature of your request." The eye blinked again as it waited for a response.

Alexander glanced at the equipment that lined the walls and then at the eye. "Um, hi."

The eye blinked again, and the computerized voice spoke. "Request not recognized. Please state the nature of your villainous request. Acceptable responses include: bank robbery, kidnapping, murder, mayhem, littering, world domination."

A large grin spread over Alexander face. "Bank robbery."

"Acknowledged. Initiating bank robbery teleportation plan Alpha Z."

Alexander watched as machinery whirred to life. He picked up a can of spray paint and approached the door. "I could get used to this," he said as he began to spray letters on the door.

E-V-I-L V-I-L-L-A-I-N-S.

CHAPTER 10

Sky Girl appeared in the Mutardi Dimension and her world turned upside down.

One moment she was in the phone booth; the next, she was . . . somewhere else. The sudden change was disorienting. The heroine's vision filled with the multitude of colors and bright lights of the strange dimension.

"I can't get my bearings. Am I upside down?" She gasped as she inhaled the purple air.

Her lungs began to burn. "Can't breathe!" Soon she could not speak at all. She could only wheeze and cough as the toxic atmosphere continued to permeate her lungs. Sky Girl grabbed her throat as she gasped for air. A purple haze closed around her.

Her body spasmed from the lack of air as she hyperventilated.

"Stupid way to die," she was finally able to mutter into the near vacuum of Mutardi space. Sky Girl began to black out. "Should have . . . gone . . . to the bank . . . with Jason."

She passed out, her limp body floating through the pink and purple swirls in the Mutardi dimension.

Several hours later, Jason stood between two red velvet ropes leading to the teller counter at the First Bank of Colonia. He was the fourth person in line.

A very old woman up front carried a large bag of pennies. Behind her, a young mother tried to pick her son up off the floor. The three-year-old child appeared to have lost all will to move and had flopped onto the ground. Jason recognized the elderly security guard who watched the scene with interest. The smile on the guard's face showed that he had seen this type of display before. Given how long the guard had worked there, Jason wondered if he had ever witnessed him doing the same thing when he'd come there with his mother as a child.

Jason sighed. This was a stupid way to spend an afternoon. He wished he could be with DeDe. She was probably exploring the Mutardi Dimension and having the time of her life. *Bet it is breathtaking*, he thought enviously.

Jason looked out the bank window. He could see Krauzer's across the street. He smiled as he remembered how his mother would always take him to that convenience store to buy new comics when they were done at the bank. Another sudden memory hit Jason, and he took out his wallet and removed a small, plastic card. "I knew it!" Jason carefully put the card back into the wallet and the wallet into his pants.

A bell dinged, announcing the teller was open and available, and the woman with the pennies approached the counter. As she lumbered over to the open cashier window, the bank teller stared at the unwrapped coinage with a look of horror that rivaled one of the victims in the zombie movie Jason had just finished watching.

Just then, the teller's attention was drawn away as the lights in the bank flickered. A strange smell permeated Jason's nostrils. "That smells like Ozone," he mused.

Suddenly, a bright light appeared in the corner of the bank. Jason squinted as he watched the lights swirl until they formed a large tunnel made of what appeared to be solid, multicolored lights.

He recognized it immediately from his comics. "Oh, my gosh. That is a Z-Gate!"

Jason closed his eyes and tried to remember what he knew about the strange device. Professor Z used Z-Gates for infiltration. It allowed the user to travel long distances by walking through a mystical dimension.

Jason opened his eyes and looked over at the old security guard, who had taken out his weapon and pointed it at the tunnel. That's when Jason remembered another little detail about the gate.

"Watch out! It is programmed to react to threats!" Jason yelled to the guard, but he was too late.

The tunnel hummed as a tendril formed on one of its edges. The elderly security guard lost hold of his gun as the tendril, which looked like a bolt of lightning, shot out from the tunnel and wrapped around the guard's arm. He screamed in pain and slumped to the floor as he was zapped into unconsciousness. Jason could smell burnt hair.

I should be okay as long as I do not present a threat, Jason thought as he cautiously stepped toward the light vortex and peered in. In the distance, he could see the silhouette of a large light bulb. His eyes scanned the scene, and he noticed a large metal door in the distance. Someone had written the words "Evil Villain's Layer" on the door in red spray paint. He thought of a layer cake belonging to an evil villain, and then dismissed the misspelled word as silly. The door opened, and a shadowy figure with a cape walked toward him.

Jason dashed away from the tunnel and yelled to everyone in the bank, "Everyone, get back! This could get bad."

Jason squinted into the tunnel. "DeDe should have come to the bank with me," he muttered as he watched the figure walk through the tunnel and into the bank.

Jason quickly moved away from the tunnel toward the center of the bank. "Everyone remain calm. No sudden moves."

The old lady ignored him and continued to count the pennies. The teller shrieked with horror and ran out the back fire exit. The mother scooped up her child and rushed out the front doors of the bank.

"Or you could all just run," Jason mumbled under his breath.

Jason knelt down and examined the security guard on the ground. The guard looked okay, just unconscious. As he stood up, Jason kicked the gun away, hoping to avoid a repeat performance from the lightning tendril. "I hope someone will at least call the police."

Jason turned toward the tunnel, watching with a mixture of fear and excitement as the figure emerged from it. DeDe had run up against several villains in her short career as Sky Girl, but this guy was the big one: Professor Z. He was the cream of the crop, the greatest at being the worst. After all, Professor Z was the villain that had beaten SkyBoy. Jason squinted as the villain stepped into the bank from the tunnel.

An overweight, masked teenager dressed in black spandex and a black cape exited the Z-Gate. The ill-fitting spandex failed to fully cover his mid-section, and his stained white undershirt poked through. The tunnel vanished as quickly as it had formed, causing the villain to trip over his cape and sprawl out on the bank floor. As the villain regained his footing and tried to stand, Jason noticed that the fiend's cowl-like mask had shifted and sat askew, so that one eyehole was blocked.

"Aw, man!" exclaimed the villain.

Jason cleared his throat, and the teenager in spandex turned to look at him. He smiled as his eyes met the villain's uncovered one. "Um, hi. Are you a super villain?"

"Hi. And why, yes, I am," he said as he readjusted his mask. "You know, they never mention in the movies how hard it is to keep the mask on."

Jason nodded knowingly as he remembered DeDe's many complaints over the summer during their mask trials. "I know what you mean. You know, a little spirit gum will hold that thing right in place."

"Really? Spirit gum? Like the circus guys use? I hadn't thought of that. Thanks." The man smiled and then looked over at the wall. "Well, okay then. Nice meeting you. I have, you know, villainous work to do." He moved toward the vault.

Jason threw up his hands. "Wait!"

"Yeah, what?"

Jason stared at the overweight spandex-clad teen. "Um, you cannot just rob the bank."

The villain stared at him. "I cannot? I mean, I can't?"

Jason rolled his eyes. "Duh. First you have to announce your fiendish intentions and tell everyone your name." Jason looked around the bank. Only the old woman remained.

The villain appeared to think for a moment. "Well, okay then. I guess there is some merit to that." The villain took a deep breath and attempted to sound menacing as he spoke. "I'm Alex, and I'm here to rob this bank."

Jason stared at him with an annoyed look.

"What?"

"Alex? Really?"

"What's wrong with Alex?"

Jason glanced at his watch and hoped the police would be there soon. "It is a little plain. You want a name that invokes fear, like Professor Z, or Evil Brain, or Commander Chimp."

Alex pursed his lips in thought. "I know—my mother always wanted me to be a doctor. So call me Doctor Doom!"

Jason shook his head from side to side. "That name is taken by a Marvel Comics villain. Trust me, you do not want them coming after you for infringement. They are owned by Disney now."

"What about Doctor Destiny?"

"Nope. DC Comics."

"Doctor Midnight?"

"No way."

"Doctor Horrible?"

"Joss Whedon used that one. Neil Patrick Harris played him."

"You mean that Doogie Howser kid?"

"Yeah."

"I loved that show. How about Doctor Strange?"

"Marvel again."

"Doctor Evil?"

"Oh, come on. You are not even trying now."

The duo's debate was cut short by the sound of sirens. Alex peered out the bank window. "Aw man, now the police are here. I didn't even get to rob the bank."

Jason smiled. "You had better go. You do not want to face them without a name."

Alex, the nameless villain, pressed a button on his gauntlet and the tunnel reappeared. "Yeah, I don't really have any weapons either."

Jason chuckled. "Going back to your evil villain's layer?"

Alex looked confused. "You mean my evil villain's *lair*." He stressed the last word. Jason pointed into the tunnel, and Alex read his spray-painted sign. "Darn it! You know, I thought I might have spelled that wrong."

Alex raced down the tunnel as the police broke into the bank. Jason watched as the glowing lights of the Z-Gate shrank away and vanished.

Jason threw up his hands as the police approached him. He could hear the security guard began to groan his way back to consciousness. "He is gone now. I do not think he took anything."

"Did he say who he was?" asked one of the officers.

Jason smiled. "Not really."

The woman with the pennies finally turned around. "There are two hundred, thirteen dollars and eleven cents here in change."

The policemen and Jason stared at her.

"What?" the woman asked as she put her finger in her ear. The device let out a high pitch squeak, and the woman smiled. "Sorry. My hearing aides were off."

Jason gave the woman a polite smile and turned to the officer. "Can one of you guys give me a ride over to Edison after I deposit this check? I need to meet a friend."

He had finally figured out where he had seen that light bulb. It couldn't be a coincidence.

CHAPTER 11

Sky Girl's eyes slowly fluttered open. "Wha' happened?" She felt something crinkling under her and realized that she was lying on a bed of leaves. Putting her hands to her face, she realized she was still wearing her Sky Girl mask.

The super heroine slowly sat up and looked around. She was in the middle of a cave. Everything came back to her then, and she remembered what had happened in the Mutardi Dimension. "Oh, my gosh. There was no air. I must've passed out." Sky Girl took a deep breath. The air tasted like metal. "Yuck. At least I can breathe it."

A small black terrier rushed into the cave, trotted over to Sky Girl, and began to sniff her. Sky Girl cupped her purple-gloved hand under the canine's chin and gave him a scratch. "Hey boy," she cooed. "What are you doing here?" He turned away, and Sky Girl reached under and scratched his belly. "Who's a good boy?"

The dog turned back to look at her indignantly. "Madam, I have not been a wee boy for quite some time," he said with a Scottish accent.

Sky Girl stopped scratching, and the dog continued. "And madam, please remove yer hands. I don't even know ye."

She blushed as she removed her hands. "Sorry. Let me guess. You're . . ."

"Colonel Kirby of the Galactic Protectorate, at yer service, Lass." The dog made a polite bow as he leaned forward on his front paws.

Sky Girl returned the bow and mumbled, "With all that ridiculous information about pocket space, someone might have mentioned that the colonel was a pooch."

Kirby ignored her, stood up on his hind legs, and moved to a console. "I was quite concerned when ye arrived. Ye appeared to have more trouble than SkyBoy ever did acclimating to our Jovian environment."

Sky Girl scoffed. "There is nothing funny about it."

"Not jovial. Jovian means a gaseous planet like yer Jupiter." Kirby growled in annoyance as he leaned on the panel.

"Whatever it was, I couldn't breathe and . . ."

"Ye panicked," Kirby responded as he hit a button. A green glow covered the costumed heroine.

She stood up. "I didn't panic."

Kirby looked at the screen. "Yes, ye did. But do not worry. There are no negative effects. Just be better next time."

Sky Girl took a step towards Kirby, "Be better next time? Who the he—"

Kirby cut her off again. "Listen I am not a fan of yer father, no matter what he did. And I am certainly not a fan of ye."

Sky Girl was hurt. Everybody she had met had loved SkyBoy—well, except for the bad guys. Kirby was different. He couldn't stand him. "Fine," she snapped. "Let's just finish my mission, and I can get out of here." She took a deep breath and looked down at the dog. "The Protectorate sent me to find you. You never checked in."

Kirby turned another knob without looking up. "Yes. I was kidnapped by the KitKatKrusade. But I escaped. I was on my way to report in when I found you floating in the Mutardi Dimension like a useless chew toy." Sky Girl started to speak, but Kirby continued. "As long as yer here, perhaps ye can be of some use. I detected the unauthorized use of Z technology on Earth. It's shielded, but if I can find the source, ye can get it and bring it back to me."

Sky Girl blew on the piece of hair that had fallen into her face. "Great, now you want me to go fetch."

Kirby made barking noises as he chuckled.

CHAPTER 12

A police car pulled into the driveway of 37 Christie Street. Jason sat in the back seat and stared out the window at the large electric light bulb on top of the Edison Tower. It was still impressive after all the years it had been there.

"I don't think it's open today, son. You sure you want us to leave you here?" the older officer asked.

Jason smiled warmly. "It is okay. I am meeting a friend."

"Suit yourself."

Jason jumped out of the back seat of the squad car and closed the door, and the car pulled out of the driveway.

Jason stood on the sidewalk and waved goodbye to the policemen. He watched as the squad car drove away, becoming smaller and smaller as it moved into the distance. He would have asked for the officers' help, but he doubted they would have believed him. He smiled. "If it had not been for my recent adventures with DeDe, I would not have believed it myself."

The teen continued to walk around to the side of the building until he reached the phone booth. He pushed open the door and squeezed into the cramped booth.

"Okay, time to think." Jason knew that if he dialed the code Boosadah had given DeDe, he would end up in the other dimension. "That would be bad, since I know I cannot breathe the air there. Luckily, that is not the only code I know."

Jason knew that code sounded familiar. It wasn't until he was at the bank that he remembered where he'd seen it. When he'd seen the Krausers', he had thought about one of his earliest comic book memories. He'd been in the convenience store with his mother. After much begging, his mother finally bought him a copy of *SkyBoy Presents: Colonel Kirby's Canine Cavalcade*. The book contained a series of short adventures and games starring the intergalactic mongrel. Jason had read that book until the pages were worn out. He remembered his joy when he recently found a nearly mint copy at the New Jersey Comic Con. It even had a pristine copy of the special laminated collector card with the "Kirby Contact Codes." When Jason was little, he would carry that card everywhere and dialed the numbers in every pay phone he found. In fact, out of nostalgia, Jason still carried a copy of the card in his wallet. He had taken the card out in the bank.

Jason removed it from his wallet and ran his finger down the numbers until he found 353-7872, the number Boosadah had given DeDe. Once he located the number, he traced the dots across the page to see that the number was labeled "Transport to Mutardi Dimension Code."

Jason put the small card down on the shelf in the booth and picked up the phone. He traced his finger down the card until he found the code for "Kirby's Canine Camp" (388-2498) and dialed the number. Hopefully, the code, like so many other comic book elements he had discovered, was more than mere fiction.

On the fifth ring, a voice with a Scottish brogue answered the phone. "Who is this? How did ye get this number?"

"Is this Colonel Kirby?" Jason asked.

"Aye. Who is this?"

Jason smiled. Since Kirby was a Scottish terrier, the accent made sense. "Um, my name is Jason. Can I, um, talk to Sky Girl for a second?"

There was silence on the other side. Finally, Kirby sighed loudly and said, "I guess. Hold the line."

Jason could hear the awkward conversation on the other end of the telephone line.

Kirby sounded annoyed. "Apparently, it's for ye, lass. This ain't a barkin' answering service."

Jason could hear the tension in DeDe's voice. "Don't look at me. I didn't give it out. I don't even know your number."

DeDe picked up the receiver then and gave a weary, "Hello?"

"Hey, DeDe." Jason chirped. "Is everything okay? You sound a little upset."

"Jason? How did you . . .?" Her tone become cheerier as her spirits lifted at the sound of his voice. The thought of that made him smile. "You know what? I don't want to know."

"I told you that I am full of surprises." Jason beamed. "Are you almost done there? I had a run in with a new bad guy at the bank and—"

Sky Girl sighed. "That is so unfair. I go to outer space—" Jason heard a voice in the background correct her. "—sorry, pocket space. Whatevs! I come all the way out here and you find a bad guy at the bank."

Jason chuckled. "He was kind of harmless, but I think he was using some of Professor Z's equipment."

"Well, Colonel Kirby, who is a dog by the way—thanks for the heads up—is looking for his equipment right now."

"Great! Come back and we can look for it together." Jason smiled at the thought of teaming up with the great Colonel Kirby.

"I can't," Sky Girl mumbled.

"Why not?"

She lowered her voice to a whisper. "I'm not allowed to leave until Kirby finds the equipment and I . . ."

"And you what?" Jason asked in confusion.

"And I fetch it for him and bring it back here."

Jason laughed.

"It's not funny. And why didn't you warn me that Kirby hates SkyBoy?"

"Um, because Kirby does not hate SkyBoy. In fact, they had their own team-up book: *SkyBoy's Best Friend*. There was even a fifth week event where—"

"Well, he hates him now." Sky Girl interrupted. She lowered her voice and spoke in a dejected tone, "And me, too."

Jason wanted to console DeDe, but he heard Kirby bark in the background.

Sky Girl sniffed. "I've got to go. I need to get yelled at or something." Then the line went dead.

"That was odd," Jason mused as he looked out of the phone booth's window. "Why would Kirby hate DeDe?" Before he could give it further thought, Jason noticed the open metal door that floated a foot off the ground.

He recognized the red lettering on the door, which had previously said *Evil Villain's Layer*. Now, however, the word "Liar" was written in red spray paint above the crossed-out "Layer."

"He got closer. I guess the third time will be the charm." Jason chuckled as he opened the phone booth and approached the floating door. "Here goes nothing."

#

Kirby paced the floor of the command center, his nails clicking on the hard cement. "Of all the irresponsible, inane, stunts. Getting a phone call from yer boyfriend in the middle of a mission!"

Sky Girl sat cross-legged in the center of the room, hovering two feet off the ground. She scowled at the little dog. "He is not my boyfriend. He called because . . ."

"Because yer a rank amateur and he is an arrogant, insolent imbecile. That's why." Kirby growled. "If someone traced that signal back to this camp, we could all be doomed."

"He knows what he's doing," Sky Girl said in defense of her best friend. "He said he found some of Professor Z's equipment, maybe that's—"

"Oh!" Kirby stood up on his hind legs. "I'm sorry. I didn't realize that yer friend was better than this entire room of equipment at tracking down the unique energy signature used by Professor Z."

"But, he found—"

"I don't want to hear it." Kirby stormed out of the room.

"I am not going to let a stupid dog make me cry," DeDe protested, but she knew it was too late. She felt the tears well up in her eyes. She covered them with her purple gloved hands and hoped Kirby didn't come back to see her. "I hope Jason doesn't do anything crazy."

#

Back on earth, Jason entered the long hallway that led into the lair. Jason recognized some of Professor Z's earlier devices.

There was a half-dissected Z-blaster on a table and a helmet that said *Forget-Z-Not* hanging in the corner. Finally, Jason found exactly what he was looking for: a large device with the name *Cloaking Z-vice* stenciled onto it. Jason was grateful that yet another comic book cliché was true—villains and heroes really did label their devices and souvenirs. Jason examined the device.

There were no knobs or dials on the Cloaking Z-vice. It was just a square metal box with pulsating lights. "This must be why Colonel Kirby cannot find this place," Jason mused. "I wonder how you turn it off."

In response, a computerized eye dropped from the ceiling and said in a robotic voice, "Device is voice-activated."

"Voice-activated. So all I have to do is tell you to shut it off?" Jason asked. This would be easier than he thought.

"Negative. Only the master's voice will initiate commands."

"The master?" Jason asked.

Suddenly, a voice boomed through the room "Who dares enter my Evil Lair?" Alexander strode into the room then, still covered in ill-fitting spandex and a long black cape. When he saw Jason, his eyes lit up and he smiled. "Oh, dude. It's you."

The computer voice responded, "Master's voice recognized. Please select crime: mayhem, murder, littering, or world domination."

Jason had an idea. He turned to Alex. "Thank Rao. I thought I had lost you in the bank. I have been looking all over for you. They sent me to help you become a better villain."

Alexander looked confused. "Who sent you?"

Jason thought for a moment. "Um, The Bureau Administering Destruction, um, Gradually Until You Surrender. You know, the B.A.D. G.U.Y.S."

"Wow, the bad guys sent you?" Alexander asked hopefully.

Jason smirked. "That is correct. The, um, B.A.D. G.U.Y.S. see that there is a lot of potential here. So what do you say?"

An evil grin formed on Alexander's face. "Let's begin."

CHAPTER 13

Kirby sat in the corner and stared at Sky Girl. She did her best to ignore him as she looked out the window into the Mutardi Dimension. The purple gas twisted and swirled in the breeze. She thought about her friend Jason and hoped he wasn't doing anything too crazy.

#

Back in Professor Z's hidden laboratory, Jason had moved a large blackboard covered in lines and circles to the center of the room. He was holding a pointer and had written the words *Diabolical Plan* on it in large letters across the top. In smaller letters were the words *Nom de guerre, Nefarious laugh,* and *The Importance of a Good Monologue.* On the right hand side was written *Doctor* _____ with several words crossed out underneath. Alexander sat on a chair and stared at his would-be teacher.

Jason took a deep breath and exhaled slowly. "So that is what there is. Do you have any questions?"

Alex shrugged. Finally, he spoke. "Wow. This is a lot harder than I thought." He stood and paced. "I thought it would all be world domination and giant robots."

A computerized voice repeated his words. "World domination—Giant robots. Commencing construction."

Alexander smiled.

The machinery hummed to life as the computer began to construct what Jason could only guess would be a giant robot. He hoped he had stalled enough. "Good work, Alex. I knew you could do it. I think you are ready to make your big debut and announce your demands."

Jason brought Alexander over to face a large camera. He stood behind it and said, "Tell it to start taping." Jason typed "388-2498" on a keyboard near the camera.

Alexander looked confused. Jason tried to help. "Just say 'Commence broadcast' or something."

Alexander smiled. "Okay, cool. Commence . . ."

Jason threw his arms up. "Wait!"

"What?"

"It is that cape; it looks filthy. You have been dragging it all around this dirty laboratory." He picked up the black, tattered cape. "Let me help you take it off." Jason reached for the neck clasp and pulled hard, but it wouldn't budge. "I think it is stuck."

Jason moved back to the camera and thought for a moment. He snapped his fingers. "I know. I bet it is voice-activated like everything else around here. Try this." He whispered the hopefully correct words into Alex's ear.

Alex stood up tall and spoke in a commanding voice. "Cloak disengage!"

A computerized voice repeated the command. "Cloak disengaged."

Jason unclasped the latch and pulled off the cape.

#

Meanwhile, far away in pocket space, Kirby's machines blared to life. The dog jumped onto his hind legs and rushed to the machine. His paws appeared as two blurs as he quickly made his adjustments. "We've got it, girlie. Get ready. I just need to calibrate . . ."

Just then, a view screen came to life, and an overweight masked man appeared on the screen. He cleared his throat and spoke, reading from white index cards. "Citizens of Earth, I will take over your pitiful planet. You will rue that day you . . ." A second later the figure looked up from the cards off-screen and whined, "Rue? That sounds silly. Are you sure that thing is even on?"

Sky Girl smiled when she heard her best friend's voice off camera. "No, no. It is working. See? The red light is on. You are doing great. Tell them about the giant robots just like I wrote down for you."

The villain spoke again in a commanding voice. "And you will never be able to stop my attack from the Edison Lighthouse—" He picked up a piece of paper and began to read. "—because you do not possess the Sky Pulse necessary to hit them in the head where their main control mechanisms are located. Wow, that was really specific. That is all."

The screen went blank.

Kirby turned to Sky Girl. "Did he just tell us his location?"

Sky Girl beamed. "Yup. Jason is like that. He's kind of a big deal."

Kirby got down on all fours and stammered, "And he, but he . . ."

Sky Girl smiled wider as she adjusted her cape. "I believe the words you are looking for are 'and he got the villain to tell us exactly what to expect and how to defeat them.' Yep, he did that too. That's my best friend. He's kind of like swimming in a pool of awesome filled with waves of geekiness. Not bad for an 'arrogant insolent imbecile.'"

Sky Girl moved closer to the door and turned back to Kirby with a wry smile. "You coming?" She patted her gloved hands against her thighs and said in a high-pitched excited voice, "Come on, boy. Let's go! Let's go get the bad man."

Sky Girl wasn't sure, but she thought she saw Kirby blush before he followed her to the door.

CHAPTER 14

Twenty minutes later, Alexander sat on the floor of the warehouse and sulked. His hands were cuffed behind his back, and there was a gag on his mouth. He looked at the remains of the shattered and smoldering robots that surrounded him, unable to believe how quickly he had been defeated by Sky Girl. It was like she'd known exactly how to stop his robots. Alexander smiled under his gag. He could at least take solace in the fact that his friend and mentor, Jason, had escaped, and that the bad guys were probably on their way to rescue him now.

In the next room, Jason and DeDe sat down at a bridge table. Tears of laughter streamed down Sky Girl's face as she tried to catch her breath. "No, really. You said you were from the Bureau Administering Destruction Gradually Until You Surrender—the B.A.D. G.U.Y.S.? And he bought it?"

Jason grinned. "Hook, line, and sinker. He was not the sharpest knife in the drawer. He is probably sitting in there waiting for them to rescue him."

Sky Girl snorted. "Sounds like a tool."

Kirby growled as he picked up a deck of cards. "Are we going to keep talking about this, or are we going to play? I need to win some of my credits back."

Sky Girl stood up. "As much as fun the whole dogs-playing-poker thing was, Jason and I should be getting home."

"But, I wanted to try to get some of my money back," Jason said with a pouted.

Kirby laughed. "No, lad. Sky Girl is right. We have work to do."

"What is going to happen to Alexander?" asked Jason.

Kirby jumped down from his chair. "I will bring him to the Protectorate, and they will pass judgment. He could receive life imprisonment—" Kirby looked uncomfortably at Sky Girl. "—or some other form of punishment that fits his crime."

Jason stood up. "Do we really have to do that? I mean it is not his fault that he found this equipment."

"We can't let him go," said Sky Girl. "He knows all about you, Jason. You could be in danger."

Kirby sighed. "I'm afraid she's right. If only there were some way we could erase his memories."

Jason smiled, "You mean like a 'Forget-Z-Not'"

Kirby barked, "Exactly."

Jason's smile widened, "Well then, I guess we have to make a quick stop in the storeroom before we leave."

\#

An hour later, Alexander rode his Segway across the lobby of the Edison Tower Museum. He looked at his watch. "Darn it. I worked through lunch again. Time flies when you're having fun."

The security guard looked out onto the lawn in front of the lighthouse, where a red-haired teenager and a lanky blond kid were playing with their dog. He was about to go out and yell at them for trespassing when he realized that there was something familiar about them. He shook his head. "I'm being crazy. If they're still there after lunch, I'll handle it then."

Outside, DeDe used her SkyHearing and SkyVision to relay the activity in the lobby to Kirby and Jason. "Sounds like it worked."

Kirby looked up at the pair. "Of course it did. Ye two make quite a team. I dare say that together, ye nearly rival the effectiveness of the original SkyBoy." He put his head down. "And I apologize for my behavior earlier. I hope ye can forgive me."

DeDe smiled and bent down to Kirby. "Close the door to the lab and we'll call it even." She kissed him on the cheek.

Jason sat on the grass next to the dog. "How did it open in the first place?"

"Apparently, the genetic locks were triggered." Kirby's collar lit up as he spoke, and a portal began to appear in front of him.

Jason's eyes widened in amazement, both at the dog's words and the newly formed portal. "Genetic locks? Wow, I cannot believe Alexander is related to Professor Z."

"He isn't. There is no relationship between Security Guard Luthor and Professor Z." Kirby entered the tunnel and he, along with the tunnel, vanished.

Jason slapped his head in realization.

"You know what he was talking about?" DeDe asked.

"Huh? I have no idea. But I just realized Alexander Luthor already had a great super-villain name."

DeDe playfully smacked the back of Jason's head. "You are such a dork."

CHAPTER 15

One Month Later

DeDe looked out the classroom window. Even without using her SkyVision, she could see the football field through the classroom window. Over the past several weeks, the festival rides had been removed. There were several students on the grass.

In the front of the room, barely noticed by DeDe, Mr. Parker droned on about Aldous Huxley's *Brave New World*.

Jason sat next to DeDe, flipping through a magazine he had hidden in the middle of his book. He glanced over at his best friend and saw her intense stare, then followed her gaze out the window.

"Wow, they have almost finished rebuilding the gym," he said.

"Huh?" DeDe said dreamily.

Jason looked again and saw that DeDe wasn't looking at the gymnasium at all. The football team was running laps around the track. Jason knew exactly where DeDe's attention would be directed. He scanned the crowd until he saw Adam. The team captain and current object of DeDe's attention led the pack. His tight white shirt and red shorts were drenched with sweat. Jason rolled his eyes and looked around the room. DeDe was not the only girl in the class watching the show. He rolled his eyes again and muttered, "What is so great about jocks?" When he didn't receive an answer, he went back to reading his magazine.

Apparently, Mr. Parker had also noticed the distracted gazes of the female population of his class. He continued his lecture on the need for societal repression as he walked to the window and closed the shades. Jason tried not smile as DeDe sighed loudly.

To her credit, DeDe did open her book and tried to follow the class lecture. But it only took a few minutes before her head began to droop. A single strand of red hair fell in her face. She blew the stray hair away and returned to the book.

After another minute, she gave up and leaned over to Jason. "I am hopelessly bored out of my mind. I'm getting out of here."

"DeDe! You will get into trouble," Jason whispered harshly.

But it was too late. DeDe had already closed her eyes and concentrated.

* * *

When she opened her blue eyes again, DeDe was in the heart of the Galactic Protectorate. It was immediately clear that she had interrupted something. Gronk was talking to Boosadah. And while the teen could not understand him, the conversation was obviously intense. As soon as Boosadah noticed DeDe, the alien raised a single finger and ended the conversation. Unsatisfied with the resolution of the argument, Gronk stormed away.

"Hey," DeDe said cheerfully in an attempt to break the tension. "Wassup?"

"To what do we owe the pleasure of this school-time visit, Miss Christopher?" Boosadah asked.

"I just wanted to ask if you'd found out anything about that creature I fought last month. You know—Optimus MechApe," she added uncomfortably. Jason had come up with the name, but DeDe wasn't sold on it.

"We have found nothing further," the lizard woman responded. "I informed you of that yesterday."

"I, uh, was just following up," DeDe said as she shuffled her feet.

"How very diligent of you. I assume Mr. Parker's incredibly boring lecture on Brave New World had nothing to do with it."

DeDe stared at the ground.

"Still, while you are here, perhaps there is something we can do."

"Are we going to talk about my Dad?" DeDe asked hopefully.

Boosadah frowned. "I'm sorry; it is not yet time for that conversation. Instead, I was hoping I could show you how to use a new power. I think you are ready."

"Really?" DeDe beamed, and thoughts of her father drifted away. Her previous practices had been limited to established abilities. Jason had told her that SkyBoy had an encyclopedia of powers. He often wondered how many DeDe would develop and how many were fictional creations invented by SkyBoy's ever-changing stable of authors in what he referred to deus ex machine plot devices.

"It is called an 'electronet,' and it is tied to your emotions."

DeDe smiled as she sat back and listened more intently than she ever had in any of Mr. Parker's classes.

At Boosadah's instruction, DeDe moved to the middle of the chamber with her hands extended in front of her. Boosadah spoke softly, "The net is *a physical manifestation of extreme emotions like love. Let us try it. Think of a strong emotion."*

A small sheen of sweat appeared on DeDe's brow as she concentrated on her feelings for her father. She thought about the sadness she felt at his absence. A tiny, shimmering net appeared in the center of the room.

"I did it!" DeDe screeched. Her concentration broke, and the net vanished.

"Very good," said Boosadah. "The net was small, but with practice, it should become bigger. Remember: it is about the power of emotion. Strong emotions make stronger nets. Next time, we will see how strong it is."

"Next time?" DeDe whined.

Boosadah pressed a now familiar button. "You are being called on." The lights became brighter. Boosadah smiled and added, "The answer is irony."

A confused DeDe closed her eyes to avoid the bright lights.

CHAPTER 16

Back in English class, DeDe opened her eyes to see Mr. Parker standing at her desk.

"Well, Miss Christopher?"

Everyone stared at her.

"We are waiting for you to amaze us with your answer."

"Um . . ." DeDe cleared her throat. "Is the answer irony?"

"Exactly," Mr. Parker said excitedly as he turned to write the word in a chart on the whiteboard. "At least someone understands the material."

"I do not know how you did it, but nice save," Jason whispered.

"Thanks." DeDe blushed. Boosadah had really come through that time. After a second, she leaned over to Jason to gloat. "I learned a new power."

"Yeah, sleep-listening." Jason laughed.

"No, silly. Like a real one. Wait—is sleep-listening a power? I mean—" She checked to make sure no one was eavesdropping. Satisfied they weren't, DeDe lowered her voice to mimic Sky Girl's. "I mean a new power."

"Really? Which one? Skybreath?" Jason asked excitedly.

"Ew! No. I don't even want to know what that is. I learned electrolysis-something-or-other." She strained trying to remember the name. "Whatevs. I made a net. It was all shimmery," she said proudly.

"Electronet?" Jason offered.

"Yeah. That's the one. It was only a little net, but Boosadah said that if I practice, my electronary thing will get bigger."

"Electronet," Jason corrected.

"Why can't they just call it a SkyNet like everything else?" DeDe asked, once again blowing at a strand of hair.

"Because that is an evil computer from the future that sends indestructible killer robots that look like Austrian bodybuilders back in time to terminate the parents of the future resistance movement leader."

DeDe gave him a puzzled look.

"Hasta la copyright, babee!" he said in a heavy Austrian accent.

DeDe rolled her eyes. "I have the weirdest best friend in the world."

Jason opened his mouth to explain himself, but then decided to change the subject. He looked toward the front of the room and waited. Then, when Mr. Parker turned around to write a particularly long paragraph from the book on the board, Jason took the opportunity to quickly shove his magazine in front of DeDe.

DeDe picked up the small paper magazine. It was the latest copy of a tabloid called *The Weird World Weekly*. The headline read: "Aliens are stealing our dead."

DeDe gave Jason a curious look. "I'll ask them, but I don't think the Galactic Protectorate are taking our dead. Unless they want to learn how to become even more boring than they already are."

"Not that one. Below it." Jason leaned over and pointed out the article on the bottom left corner of the paper. "This one."

DeDe followed his finger. Printed in 22-point bold type were the words, "Jersey Devil Found." The article underneath described an eyewitness account of an encounter with the monster. There was even a grainy picture of a creature with a head like a collie and a face like a horse. The creature had a long neck, wings, and back legs like a crane's, but with a horse's hooves.

DeDe wrinkled her nose. "I'm still confused." She brushed another stray strand of hair out of her face and turned to Jason.

He smiled as he held up a copy of a comic book. Of course, Jason had put it in a small Mylar bag. But before she could mock him, she looked more closely at the book and understood.

DeDe examined the cover and recognized it as one of the books Gronk had given her at the end of the summer. The book was titled *SkyBoy Team-Up*. There was a small picture of SkyBoy in the left hand corner of the book, right above the issue number, price, and date. DeDe had noticed that a lot of comics had this little box, as if having the character's name on the cover wasn't enough for people to know who was in the book. She glanced at the number and date. It was issue number twenty-eight and about ten years old. The color had faded a bit, but it was still in pretty good shape. Under the title were the words, "This Boy, This Monster." Jason's finger lingered over a figure that took up most of the cover. DeDe examined it and then the magazine on her desk. The similarity between the two made her swallow hard.

"Ah?" Jason whispered. "You see my point?" The drawing on the comic book and the photo in the magazine were identical.

DeDe made a confused gesture.

The bell rang, signaling the end of class. Jason carefully placed the comic in his bag and walked over to DeDe's desk.

She slipped her purple backpack on and looked up at him. "I don't get it. So what's the deal? Are we in the monster-fighting business? What, do you want to be my watcher now?"

"Was that a geek culture reference?" Jason smiled. "There is hope for you yet, my young Padawan."

DeDe shot him an annoyed look. "Don't push it."

"You do not understand. Jersey Devil is not a villain. He was a misunderstood monster. He was stranded in a dimension not of his making that he did not understand. He was also—"

"Stranded in a dimension not of his making that he did not understand? Not too dramatic." She sighed.

Jason frowned. "Too dramatic? That is a classic description. It was inside every one of his books."

"Wow, every book? Oh, then I guess that makes it less corny." She gave Jason a playful shove. "But you digress. Go ahead, geek boy. Jersey Devil was also what?"

"I am not going to tell you now—geek boy, indeed."

DeDe moved closer and smiled menacingly. "You'd better tell me, or you'll feel the wrath of my other new power—the power of my SkyTickling." She pushed her finger under Jason's ribcage.

"Stop that!" He laughed. "Someone will hear us."

DeDe continued her tickling, and Jason turned red. "Feel my sky power!" She giggled.

"Okay, okay, I give," Jason finally said, out of breath. "Jersey Devil was good friends with SkyBoy. He was kind of like his confidant."

"His what?"

Jason sighed. "Confidant. The guy SkyBoy would tell his secrets and problems to. There is a chance that your father may have just used Jersey Devil as a literary device so the audience could understand SkyBoy's angst, but . . ."

"Boring."

"But, if it really happened, he may—"

"Be able to tell me more about my dad," DeDe finished as her eyes lit up.

"Speaking of, did you learn anymore about your father when you were. . ." Another student walked by, and Jason pointed to his head and made a birdie motion with his hands. DeDe laughed at his pathetic pantomime. He frowned.

Once the student had passed, DeDe continued in a hushed whisper. "She wouldn't tell me anything about my dad . . . again. At least I learned that net thingy."

"Electronet," Jason corrected and smiled. "We should just call you Thingy Girl. That is how you refer to all your powers."

"Whatevs." She absently-minded brushed stray locks of hair from her face. "I'm not very good at it; it takes a lot of concentration." When the hair fell again, DeDe tried to blow it away.

"I can see how that could be a problem." Jason laughed, watching her blow red hair into the air.

"Maybe I should just . . ." She imitated his ridiculous hand motion. "Or do you want the SkyTickling punishment to return?"

"Mercy, mercy!" Jason threw his hands up in feigned submission. "I yield before your powerful SkyTickles, Thingy Girl."

The pair laughed in the hallway, receiving strange looks from the passersby.

After Jason caught his breath, he spoke in a more serious tone. "I really think we should check out the Jersey Devil angle. We could take that tent we used in the backyard when we were kids and went camping."

"Yeah, camping," DeDe replied grudgingly. It was hardly camping. She remembered those cold nights when Jason would stay up late and read his comic books while she tried to sleep. Those nights were cold, wet, and smelly. When Jason would finally fall asleep, she would sneak back into the house and set her alarm so she could get back out before he got up. DeDe hated those nights and that tent. She only did them because Jason loved it so much. "Can't we stay in a hotel instead?"

"A hotel? In the woods?" Jason asked in surprise. "There are no hotels in the woods."

DeDe sensed his mocking tone and angrily turned towards him.

The impending argument was interrupted by Adam as the muscular quarterback approached the pair. As usual, Nicole invaded Adam's personal space as she stood next to him, her arm intertwined with his. DeDe lost track of the argument when she saw them. She didn't look happy to see the couple as she glared at the encircled arms as if willing them apart.

Jason wasn't sure if it was his imagination, but Adam also appeared discontented with Nicole's public display of affection.

"Hey, guys. What's up?" Adam said as he smiled a big toothy grin at DeDe. She blushed as she returned a goofy grin.

Jason watched Nicole cling more tightly to her boyfriend. Adam ignored her. "Hey, DeDe. Whatcha got there?"

DeDe gave Adam a shy, "Hey," in return. She fumbled with the copy of the *Weird World Weekly* and showed the magazine to Adam, pointing to the picture. "Jason and I are going camping and monster hunting this weekend." She immediately winced when she realized how silly it sounded.

Adam took the magazine and glanced at the cover article. "The Jersey Devil. Cool."

"Be vewy, vewy quiet. We're hunting Devils," Jason joked.

No one laughed. Nicole sighed loudly, and DeDe shot Jason a *please shut up* look.

Adam looked up from the magazine. "You know, my folks have a cabin out in the woods. Nicole and I are going this weekend. If you guys want to come with us, we could hunt together."

Nicole shot Adam the same look DeDe had just given Jason.

"No, thanks." Jason added quickly. "We have a tent and have it cover—"

"That sounds great!" DeDe interrupted as she stepped in front of Jason. To Adam, she mouthed the words, "I hate that tent."

Adam smiled. "Perfect, then."

"Fine!" Nicole blurted out, making everyone jump. "We'll meet at my house tomorrow morning at nine a.m. sharp! Don't be late, or I will leave without you." She turned and stormed away.

"Uh," Adam stammered, "she must be, um, late for class." The second bell rang.

"So are we," Jason said as he grabbed DeDe's arm. "Come on!"

DeDe waved shyly at Adam as Jason pulled her down the hallway to chemistry class.

Adam returned the wave with a big grin. When DeDe and Jason were out of sight, Adam rushed to the stairs that led down to the newly constructed gymnasium locker room.

#

The final bell rang.

The formerly crowded hallway was quiet for a moment, then one of the lockers slowly swung open to reveal a hidden passageway behind it. Candlelight flickered from inside the opening onto the floor of the hallway.

A moment later, Mr. Dennis Parker stepped out of the shadows of the secret entrance and into the hallway. "Jersey Devil? At last!"

He turned and pressed a hidden button, closing the faux locker and sealing the passageway. Then the English professor turned and raced toward Principal Vilbran's office.

CHAPTER 17

Dennis Parker rushed down the hall toward Principal Vilbran's office. His wing-tipped shoes clicked loudly on the linoleum floors and echoed off the lockers in the empty hallway. He passed the empty secretarial station outside the main office and approached the door labeled *Principal Edward Vilbran*.

Inside the office, Principal Vilbran sat at his desk and examined the woman standing before him. Miss Backerchase had been with him since the beginning. She was a tall, leggy woman with long blonde hair, which he knew she dyed especially for him. He also liked the fact that she wore too much makeup and dressed provocatively.

"Now, Miss Backerchase," Vilbran announced. "I do believe it is time for our afternoon session."

Miss Backerchase picked up a dictation notebook and moved to sit on the desk next to Vilbran.

The office door flew open, and Miss Backerchase gasped as she turned. She threw her hands up in an exaggerated gesture and sighed as she dropped the notebook back on the desk.

"We need to talk. Now!" the wily English professor announced as he stormed into the room.

Vilbran gave Parker an annoyed look. The principal slowly stood and turned to the leggy secretary sitting on his desk. "We will continue this later, Miss Backerchase. For now, see that we are not disturbed, no matter what you hear."

"Yes sir, Principal Vilbran, sir." Miss Backerchase said in a high-pitched voice and a thick Bronx accent as she closed the door and left the office.

Vilbran stood silently for a moment. He sighed loudly and turned to Mr. Parker.

Their eyes met for a moment before Parker broke the gaze and stared at the floor.

Vilbran sighed again, this time louder. "Mr. Parker . . ."

"Sorry, sir. I sometimes get excited and—"

"Enough, Jimmy!" The force of his voice was enough to make the English teacher jump. "What is so important that you would interrupt my daily dictation?"

Mr. Parker looked at the door through which Miss Backerchase had exited. "Ah, yes. I will get straight to the point. I was in the passages behind the lockers on my way to read more dictionaries—you know how I spend my afternoons researching my—"

Vilbran was becoming annoyed. "If there is a point, I suggest you find it soon."

"I overhead several students discussing the location of Jersey Devil."

"Fascinating. Perhaps you can start an on-campus crypto-zoology society and discuss Bigfoot, the Loch Ness Monster, and—"

"They mentioned SkyBoy's connection to him."

"Which students?" Vilbran snarled.

"I was sure I heard Mr. Berg and Miss Debis. I think there were others."

"Miss Debis? Excellent. That will be all, Jimmy," Vilbran said as he dismissed the English teacher, but Mr. Parker did not leave.

"But sir," Parker added, "if they have found Jersey Devil, he may be able to help me with—" He searched for the right word . "—my situation."

"Very well. You may follow them." Mr. Parker became elated at Vilbran's words. The principal added in a commanding voice, "But only to observe. Take Miss Trojakowski with you."

Mr. Parker looked confused. "The new chemistry teacher?"

Vilbran's voice was strained with annoyance. "Yes! Her unique skill set may prove useful in this endeavor."

Vilbran waved his hand in dismissal.

Mr. Parker bowed as he left the office. "I shall do my best."

Vilbran looked out his window and pondered the situation for a moment. He pressed the red button on his desk and summoned Miss Backerchase. Almost immediately, the buxom assistant came in. Before she could speak, Vilbran ordered, "Get me Judge Debis on the phone. I need to talk to him about his daughter." She nodded and turned to leave. He quickly added in a softer tone, "And after that we can continue with our daily tasks, Miss Backerchase."

Backerchase gave a shy smile and squeaked. "Yes sir, Principal Vilbran. Right away, Mr. Vilbran." She left the office and closed the door quietly behind her.

Vilbran turned back to the window and mulled over the latest turn of events. "Perhaps things are finally falling into place," he said to an empty room.

CHAPTER 18

The next morning, DeDe and Jason stood on the sidewalk in front of 9102 New Dover Road, the Debis residence. Although at 12,000 square feet, it wasn't really fair to refer to it as a house. Nicole lived in the prestigious estate area of Colonia. Rumor had it that the star of a famous fifties sitcom, had once lived in this large house. DeDe was sure that Nicole had started the rumor.

Jason examined the outside of the large mansion. Although the sun shone brightly, the house still appeared eerily dark. Overgrown ivy snaked around large black columns on the porch. Large bay windows overlooked the driveway. Jason peered up at one of the windows. He could see Nicole's mother as she stood in the window and stared at them. Despite the distance, Jason could see that she was stunning, an attractive older woman with a very exotic look.

Back when they were still friends with Nicole, Jason and DeDe often debated the country of her mother's origin. Apparently, she had been a jet-setting supermodel before she'd married the Honorable Caesar Debis and settled down in

Colonia. Even now, as she stood in the window and glared, she wore a revealing purple negligee.

The woman scowled at them, and Jason once again thought that Mrs. Debis would have been truly beautiful woman, except for the fact that she always looked so grim. There was deadness to her eyes, as if she had lost something very important. In the entire time he'd known her, Jason had never seen the woman smile.

He leaned over to DeDe. "It appears we have an audience." He waved at the older woman in the window. Mrs. Debis gave him another stern scowl before closing the curtain. "Nice to know some things never change."

"Like mother, like daughter," DeDe replied as she watched Nicole leave the house with Adam with the same scowl on her face.

"You're late. We were going to leave without you," Nicole said as she opened the car door.

"Well, I am glad you decided to wait," Jason said as he climbed into the back seat.

"Who said I decided to wait?" Nicole said with practiced indifference as she got into the driver's seat and slid it as far back as it would go. The back of the seat slammed into Jason's legs and left him with no room.

"She's kidding," Adam said with a smile as he opened the passenger side door. He gestured to the open door. "After you, milady."

DeDe blushed. "Thanks, Adam."

Adam glanced at Jason's crushed feet in the small back seat. "Um, unless you would rather sit in the front. It's bigger."

Nicole leaned over to look out of the open door at DeDe and Adam. "I don't think that would be a good idea."

DeDe glared at Nicole and then spoke to Adam softly. "Thanks for the offer. But she's probably right. You're taller than me, and I can keep Jason company."

Adam put his hand on her arm and helped DeDe in. "Suit yourself. Let me know if you or Jason want to switch."

"Roger that," DeDe said as she squeezed into the small back seat of Nicole's sports car.

Jason gave her a look and whispered, "Roger that? Seriously?"

DeDe blushed a deep shade of crimson. "Oh, just shut up." She looked down at his legs and feet, which were being crushed by Nicole's seat. "If I were you, I would just focus on thinking small thoughts. It's a long ride."

Jason just smiled as the car pulled out of the driveway and down New Dover Road towards the Garden State Parkway.

The two-hour car ride was very quiet and equally uncomfortable. Nicole and DeDe didn't talk at all. Each time Jason tried to say something, DeDe shushed him. And whenever Adam opened his mouth, Nicole gave a stern, cold look that silenced the football player. Finally, the foursome was at the end of their long, uncomfortable trek. Nicole pulled her car into a large parking lot next to a wooded area. There was an opening in the bushes and a clearly marked trail labeled *Cabins*.

"Well, here we are!" Adam said. As he got out of the car, he pressed a latch and the seat moved forward.

Jason sighed. "Well, that was fun."

DeDe elbowed her best friend, who threw his hands up in frustration.

Nicole opened her door and got out of the driver's side.

Jason moved to exit, but Nicole slammed the door on him.

"No problem, Nicole. I will get out on the passenger side. Thanks for thinking of me, though," Jason sang.

She rolled her eyes and moved to open the trunk.

DeDe and Jason crawled out of the small back seat. Jason stamped his feet and rubbed his legs in an attempt to regain the circulation in them. He then moved to the back of the car and reached into the trunk to remove his pack. He nearly toppled over with the weight of the bag. "Wow, that is heavier than I remember. I, uh, must be hungry," he muttered

"I'm sure that's it," DeDe said as she reached in with one hand and lifted her large backpack with ease. Adam stared in amazement as the tiny girl hefted the heavy bag.

Jason shot her a concerned look. "Wow, DeDe, that bag sure looks heavy."

"No, I'm—" DeDe saw Adam's surprised look then and quickly grasped the bag with both of her hands, pretending to struggle with it. "I mean, boy, this bag sure is heavy. I can barely hold it."

Jason rolled his eyes at the poor display of thespianism.

Nicole ignored DeDe and removed her designer backpack from the trunk, easily tossing it to Adam. The force and weight of the bag nearly knocked the muscular football player to the ground. He made a mental note to follow up on this later.

Adam struggled to pick up Nicole's bag. "Wow, I must be hungry too."

"Oh, please." Nicole sighed as she gave Adam a pathetic stare and picked her bag up and threw it over her shoulder.

Adam tried not to look embarrassed as he grabbed his own pack from the trunk.

If DeDe had seen the exchange, she didn't mention it, but instead looked around the campsite. "So what is this place? Where are we going?"

Adam perked up at the question and the change of subject. "This is the Jenny Jump State Park. Our camp is about a mile up the trail. It's a really scenic hike. I loved coming here with my family. We are going to walk by a bunch of trees, bushes, and caves, and then the cabin is up at the top of the hill."

"Caves?" Jason asked.

"Yeah, a whole bunch of them. They go on for miles underground. I think the most famous is called Faery Hole, but there are a whole bunch of them," Adam said proudly. "I used to explore them as a kid."

"How wonderful for you," Nicole said coldly. "We'd better move if we want to get there." She walked past them into the woods. "Watch out for rattlesnakes."

Adam gave the other two an apologetic look. "She's just, uh, concerned." He raced into the trail after Nicole.

"Yeah, concerned about herself," Jason mumbled. After he'd made sure Adam and Nicole had moved out of hearing range, he whispered to DeDe, "Jersey Devil lived in a cave."

"You think we can find him?"

"I already have a plan."

DeDe grinned. "I thought you might."

"We will wait for Adam and Nicole to fall asleep, and then we will go explore. I will set up home base in the tent."

DeDe rolled her eyes at the thought of the tent. Jason ignored her.

"And you can fly over the caves. I think maybe your SkyVision can find Jersey Devil's heat signature. Then—"

"Are you guys coming?" Adam yelled.

"Be right there!" DeDe yelled back melodically.

After a moment, Jason turned to DeDe. "You do not think she was serious about the rattlesnakes, do you?"

DeDe gave him a friendly shove. "Don't worry. I'll protect you." She disappeared onto the trail toward the source of the voice in the woods.

"Snakes. Why did it have to be snakes?"

"I heard that," DeDe chimed cheerily from the foliage. "You are such a dork."

Jason chuckled and followed his best friend into the forest.

CHAPTER 19

DeDe and Jason quickly caught up to Adam and Nicole. Jason took his position in the back of the group, watching closely as Nicole moved ahead at a breakneck pace. She appeared to have no trouble traversing the steep trail or climbing over the large rocks. Adam, on the other hand, could barely keep pace with Nicole and eventually gave up. Adam slowed his pace so that he could keep pace with DeDe. The pair walked next to each other about fifty feet ahead of Jason and talked. He tried to listen but couldn't hear them. "Man. SkyHearing would come in handy right now," he muttered.

Instead, Jason let his thoughts drift and focused on what he could remember about the Jersey Devil.

Jersey Devil was from another dimension and spoke using a weird language that consisted solely of grunts. The creature was transported to Earth's dimension by Shadow, one of the more dangerous members of SkyBoy's rogue gallery.

Jason considered Shadow. The villain had been a mainstay of SkyBoy's rogue gallery since his first appearance. A misguided mystic had brought Shadow to Earth's dimension.

Shadow was bound to the mage, which allowed him to permanently remain in this plane of existence. The demon had attempted to take over the planet time and time again. Each time, he'd been stopped by SkyBoy. Still, there had been no sign of Shadow since DeDe had discovered her powers.

When the Gorilla Army had held Jason captive, Commander Chimp had bragged that Shadow had helped him to find the Choyut Dragon. Jason wondered if Sky Girl would ever have to face Shadow and what they would do if that happened. He wasn't looking forward to it.

Jason turned his attention back to Jersey Devil. Shadow had hoped to use the powerful devil's nearly omnipotent sorcery to defeat SkyBoy. Jersey Devil refused, turned against Shadow, and became one of the good guys. However, because of his monstrous appearance and difficulty in speaking, he was never accepted by society. Instead, he was content to live in caves and exist as an urban legend. Jason didn't own the issues, but eventually, in a never reprinted comic book mini-series about the creature, Jersey Devil met a higher power who charged the creature with the responsibility to keep what Jersey Devil would later (and in every issue) refer to as the universal mystical balance. Because of this responsibility, Jersey Devil sometimes opposed SkyBoy and other heroes and even appeared to be a villain in some stories. In the end, he was always revealed to be a force for good. SkyBoy eventually learned the creature's language, and the two met at least once a year in a semi-annual crossover event. Jason loved those psychedelically cosmic stories. They reminded him of the great Silver Age comic books.

He wondered how much from the comics was true.

Jason lost his train of thought when he heard Adam's loud laugh. Now that he thought about it, Adam and DeDe had been laughing quite a bit on this walk.

"What could they be talking about that is so darn funny?" Jason wondered aloud.

A few feet ahead of Jason, Adam caught his breath after the most recent round of laughter and wiped a tear from his eyes. "You're kidding me. You guys climbed on your tricycles and pulled the fire alarms?"

DeDe smiled warmly. "Jason convinced me it was a signal that was going to call a flying rodent guy or something."

"The flying rodent guy signal. That's funny."

"Well, it didn't call him. Instead, a lot of fire trucks and police cars showed up. We watched the flashing lights from the window of my bedroom. We figured out we were in trouble and hid under the bed." DeDe smiled at the memory of her and Jason going on the lam without actually leaving the bedroom.

"What happened next?"

"My dad found us. No matter how hard I tried, I could never hide from him." DeDe's eyes started to tear up as she thought of her father. "He tried to act mad, but in some ways I think he was proud of us." She turned away from Adam and wiped a tear. "I think Dad had a really big rebellious streak."

Adam, seeing DeDe's emotion, changed the subject. "So Jason is really special, huh?"

DeDe looked back at her gawky friend. Jason had taken off his windbreaker, revealing a black t-shirt that said "Aberzombie and Witch." She smiled fondly. "He's my favorite geek in the world. I like him, and I think I'll keep him."

Adam grabbed her hands and stopped her in the middle of the path. He took a deep breath. "Well, you know who I like?"

DeDe's heart raced. What was he doing? "Who?"

Adam paused for a moment as he stared past DeDe into the woods. "Mr. Parker?"

DeDe gaped at the object of her affection. "You like Mr. Parker? The English teacher?"

"No!" Adam let go of DeDe's hands and moved off the trail toward the woods near a cave. "I thought I just saw Mr. Parker go into that cave. I think the new chemistry teacher was with him. Let's go see."

DeDe's last chemistry teacher, the evil Commander Chimp, suddenly came to mind. "Hey, wait up," she said, turning to follow him. "It could be dangerous."

But Adam had already moved near the entrance to the cave. "C'mon," he said with a grin. "They're teachers. What could happen?"

Behind them, Jason watched DeDe leave the path and rushed to catch up. "Hey, wait for me!"

In his haste, Jason didn't see the twig that blocked the path. He tripped over the branch and fell hard to the ground, grunting as he slammed his face into the cold earth. "That will leave a mark," he murmured to the ground. When he finally stood up and regained his footing, he carefully walked over to where DeDe and Adam had disappeared. He moved a tree branch just in time to see them enter a small cave.

"Hey!" he yelled again as he tried to catch up and avoid another fall.

#

Meanwhile, Nicole had already reached the cabin. She entered the dwelling and put down her pack, then opened it and removed a magazine.

Within minutes, she was sitting on the bed reading the fashion magazine, oblivious to the location of her boyfriend.

#

As Adam and DeDe entered the cave, DeDe pointed at one of the torch-lined walls. "Do you see that?" she asked.

Adam looked in the direction she indicated and saw strange symbols written in a language that neither of them recognized. "Is that a trick of the torch light, or are the symbols glowing?"

They moved further into the cave.

"That's a surprise," said Adam. "It's really well lit. I thought we were going to need the flashlight."

"We should just go," DeDe said, doing a double-take at the symbols glowing on the wall. "This is weird."

Adam grabbed her hand and squeezed. "Don't be afraid, DeDe. I'll protect you."

DeDe squeezed back and sighed as the pair walked towards the center of the cave, passing another smoking set of torches. "It's so smoky."

DeDe used her SkyVision to peer through the haze and saw two figures standing in the corner. "Wait. They're over there," she whispered as she pointed at the pair of teachers.

"Wow. You have really good eyesight," Adam whispered back.

A large cauldron sat on the far side of the cave, the fire underneath it illuminating the cave.

Ms. Tina Night Trojakowski, the new chemistry professor, peered into the black pot as Mr. Parker examined a stack of books. Miss Trojakowski was holding something very tightly. The device flashed in her hands.

Adam squinted in the dim light. "What is that? It looks like some kind of triggering mechanism."

"That looks like a dead-man trigger. Jason told me about it once."

"You guys talk about weird stuff."

She neglected to mention that she'd learned of the device during one of their many training sessions. "Shh. This is serious. He said once it's turned on, somebody has to hold on to it or it will go off."

"What would go off?"

DeDe wrinkled her brow. "I don't know. Something. All I know is that if Miss Trojakowski lets go of that thing, something is gonna go off."

"What—"

"Give me a sec." DeDe withdrew her hand from Adam's and looked back at the entrance to the cave, using her SkyVision to examine everything. The light brown contours of the cave turned a cool blue. The appearance of red blotches caused her to gasp. The cave opening was lined with explosives.

DeDe wasn't sure what was going on, but she knew Sky Girl had to stop them.

DeDe opened her backpack and put it on the ground, then straightened to her full five-foot height. She put her hands on her hips, lowered her voice and yelled, "Hey, what do you think you're doing?"

"What are *you* doing?" Adam asked.

DeDe had completely forgotten that he was standing right next to her. She quickly slouched and added in a flighty voice, "Um, is this a field trip or something?"

"Sorry, Parker. You're on your own!" Miss Trojakowski yelled as she ran past them toward the cave opening.

DeDe watched the chemistry teacher vanish through the opening. Someone else stood in the entryway, and Miss Trojakowski was on target to collide with them.

"Oh no!" DeDe exclaimed when she realized who the other party was.

Miss Trojakowski slammed into Jason, who once again fell to the ground.

The impact knocked the detonator from the chemistry teacher's hand, and it emitted a long beep as it fell to the ground.

"Jason!" DeDe shrieked.

"DeDe!" Jason yelled.

"Huh?" said Adam.

"Oh, dear." Parker sighed.

Miss Trojakowski just smiled and said, "Boom!"

And the cave entrance exploded.

CHAPTER 20

Jason felt himself being pushed by the concussive blast through the narrow opening of the cave and out into the forest. There was a loud screech. He wasn't sure if it was the ringing in his ears or Miss Trojakowski's screams.

Jason landed hard next to a tree, lying face down in the mud. He slowly forced his head up to see what had happened. That was when he first saw the creature moving towards him. His eyesight was blurry from the impact, but he could clearly see it—whatever it was—coming directly for him.

"Oh, great. This is perfect," Jason said with as much sarcasm as he could muster before he passed out, his head flopping down in the mud. The grotesque creature picked Jason up with one hand, holding him close to his horse-shaped face, and sniffed. A second later, the monster tossed the teen over his shoulder and trotted off into the woods.

CHAPTER 21

DeDe squinted against the bright lights. "What happened?" she groaned.

She was surprised to hear Boosadah's gentle voice answer her. "It was Miss Nitro. You were caught in an explosion."

"Oh, my gosh. What about Jason? And Adam?"

Boosadah spoke softly but intently. "It is Mr. Parker that you should be concerned about. If he finds his word . . ."

"Wha—?" DeDe said as the lights got brighter, a signal that she was waking up.

"Remember," Boosadah added, "keep the secret of Sky Girl safe at all costs. Beware the word."

* * *

"What word?" DeDe mumbled as she opened her eyes. Adam's face leaned in close to hers. She was lying on the hard cold floor of the cave with her head on his lap as he touched her hair.

DeDe quickly sat up.

"What word? DeDe, are you okay?" Adam asked. Embarrassment and concern lingered in his voice. "You caught that explosion full force. I mean, I think you did, but your clothes aren't even burned. You aren't even dirty." He looked down as his own soiled jeans and tattered t-shirt.

DeDe rubbed her head and tried to ignore Adam's muscles. "I'm okay. I must have—" She paused for a moment. "—um, rolled with it."

"Yeah, I guess so," Adam said and dropped the subject.

"I can't believe you bought that lame excuse," DeDe murmured.

"What?"

"Sorry. I thought I was using my inside voice. Let me see how bad it is."

DeDe stood up and looked around the cave. The opening had collapsed, and they were trapped on the inside of the cave-in. Several torches had blown out, but the cave was still lit in an eerie green glow coming from the corner of the room. In that corner, Mr. Parker sat on the floor and flipped through an oversized book. "At least Mr. Parker brought a flashlight," she muttered to herself before realizing there was no reading light. Instead, the book itself was glowing.

Mr. Parker looked up at the ceiling of the cave and yelled, "Sherriot!" When nothing happened, he turned back to the book, clearly disappointed.

DeDe turned back to Adam. "What's going on with Mr. Parker?"

"I don't know. He keeps shouting weird things. I think he's in shock," Adam said, gesturing to the English teacher. "Or he's just a kook."

DeDe remembered Boosadah's warning about Mr. Parker's word. "Yeah, we should get out of here."

"I tried. The rocks are too heavy." Adam looked hopeful. "But maybe you'll have better luck."

DeDe looked shocked "Me? Why me?" Did Adam know more than he was saying?

Adam looked embarrassed. "Um, I thought you might have an idea. You know—you're real smart and stuff."

"I'm sorry. I snapped, I'm feeling a little claustrophobic," she lied.

"Hey, we may be trapped, but at least we're in good company."

"Nardiello!" yelled Mr. Parker.

"Well, almost good company."

DeDe smiled back, and the pair laughed. Mr. Parker gave the students an annoyed look before he returned to his book.

DeDe put a hand on Adam's shoulder. "I'm sure Jason will get help and come back." She was sure that she'd seen him right before the explosion. She hoped her best friend was okay.

Mr. Parker yelled, "Hatzamachalis!"

Adam smiled as he took her hand. "Yeah, or Nicole. It's been a while. I'm sure she's starting to get worried."

Adam didn't see DeDe roll her eyes.

\#

Meanwhile at the cabin, Nicole was sound asleep in her bed, snoring loudly.

CHAPTER 22

Jason rubbed his neck and opened his eyes. He could see a rock ceiling and felt the cold earth beneath him. He was on the dirt floor of a cave. "I really need to stop waking up in strange places," he said, slowly sitting up. "How sad that I find it strangely comforting that I have not been handcuffed or placed in a death trap this time." Jason stared into the darkness. "At least I hope I am not in a death trap."

Slowly, Jason rose to his feet and strained his memory. He had seen DeDe in the cave before the explosion. "Oh, my gosh! She might still be trapped in there." He reached into his pocket to get his headset, sighing when he felt the broken pieces in his pocket. Jason slowly pulled them out. But as he had expected, the headset and receiver were smashed beyond repair. He shoved the radio headset back into his pocket and sighed.

After a moment, he looked around and decided to make the most of his situation. "Let us see what kind of mess I have gotten myself into this time."

The cave was very plain. Something on the wall caught Jason's attention, and he went to examine it. There were hash marks decorating the cave wall. For every four marks, there was a line struck through, as if someone had made the chalk markings to keep count of something.

"I hope that is not how many kids have been eaten here."

It was then that he heard a low-pitched groan from the other side of the cave. He followed the noise, which led him across the cave in the direction of a long tunnel. A light flickered in the darkness at the end of the tunnel.

"I guess there is only one way to find out." Jason slowly made his way down the tunnel toward the light. When he was about halfway across the cave he heard music in addition to the low groaning. Jason quietly entered the cave tunnel.

When he caught a glimpse of what was in the room, he quickly forgot about the groans and music.

CHAPTER 23

On the other side of the forest, Adam and DeDe sat on the cold stone floor of their own cave. DeDe knew that she could use her SkyStrength to easily get them out of the cave. The only problem was that she didn't know how to do it without Adam or Mr. Parker discovering her secret. Given Boosadah's warning, she had to be especially careful about raising their suspicions.

She looked over at her frail English Professor. He had made his way through about half of the glowing book, becoming more agitated with each word. With wild eyes, Mr. Parker yelled, "Auchterlonie!" Again, nothing happened.

DeDe turned to Adam. "I guess he's harmless enough."

Adam nodded.

Satisfied that she and Adam were not in any immediate danger, DeDe decided to wait out the situation.

Besides, despite the circumstances, she was having a great time sitting and talking with Adam. They chatted about football and school and found that they had a lot in common. Adam was warm and caring. Most exciting to DeDe was that after years of unrequited crushing, Adam was actually paying attention to her. A part of her felt somewhat selfish for enjoying it so much.

"I can't believe this place," Adam said as he looked around the cave.

"It's amazing," DeDe said with a smile as she gazed into the football player's eyes.

#

"This is amazing," Jason said as he examined a large, glowing sphere. The globe stretched six feet in diameter and floated in the center of the room. He reached out to touch it, but a loud roar froze him in his tracks.

He turned to see the ten-foot-tall Jersey Devil moving toward him.

#

Nicole slept in her comfortable bed at the cabin. She was in such a deep sleep that she didn't even hear Miss Nitro as she entered the cabin. She did not stir as the villainess rifled through Nicole's backpack. And she continued to sleep even after Miss Nitro removed the small cellular phone from the zipper pocket.

"Amazing," Miss Nitro said as she left the cabin.

Nicole turned over and continued to snore loudly.

CHAPTER 24

DeDe and Adam were enjoying their time trapped in the cave, surprisingly, trading funny stories and laughing together.

"You know," Adam said nervously when he remembered Mr. Parker in the corner. "I should really make sure he's okay." Adam stood up and brushed the dust from his pants. "If you're tired, you should take a nap first. We can take turns." He took off his varsity jersey and balled it into a pillow for her. His muscles glistened in the green glow of the cave.

DeDe looked down at the floor. "Such chivalry." Of course, she was not tired. She hadn't really gotten tired since she'd inherited her Sky powers. Still, she took the jersey from Adam. She would use this opportunity to try to get some information.

DeDe sat cross legged and meditated, closing her eyes in concentration.

* * *

When she opened her eyes again, she was in the council chamber of the Galactic Protectorate. For some reason, DeDe did not appear in the center of the room as usual. Instead, she had arrived in one of the shadowy alcoves. Nearby, Boosadah was talking to Gronk in front of a large viewscreen.

"You know—" DeDe started as she moved to approach them, but then she heard her name and decided to keep quiet.

"No, DeDe is not ready for the truth yet," Boosadah said tenderly.

"GRONK," the creature roared.

"I am sorry. You have done much, but there is still more to your sentence," Boosadah said, a touch of sadness coloring her voice.

"GRONK," the rock creature said with equal sadness.

"Deidre cannot be allowed to talk to him. She must be kept away from Jersey Devil."

The grotesque creature gestured to the wall. "GRONK!"

"I am afraid her friend Jason is on his own. She cannot learn the truth." The lizard bowed her head, and DeDe saw what was on the viewer—a split screen. On one half was an image of DeDe sitting cross legged in the cave with Adam in the background. He was trying to talk to Mr. Parker, who was doing his best to ignore him. On the other half of the screen was an image of her best friend being attacked by a ten-foot-tall monster.

"Jason!" she yelled as she stepped from her hiding place in the alcove. Boosadah jumped in surprise. Gronk quickly rose to his giant stone feet.

"What are you doing? Were you spying on us?" Boosadah demanded.

"No!" DeDe yelled with tears in her eyes. "You don't get to do this. Do not turn this on me. You are going to tell me about my father." She glanced at the screen again. "But first, I have to save my best friend."

Gronk tenderly put his hand on DeDe's shoulder, but did not understand what the creature was trying to tell her.

"GRONK!" he said, gesturing to the image of Mr. Parker.

Boosadah spoke harshly. "He is trying to tell you that Mr. Parker is the real threat, along with Miss Nitro. While you have been flirting with *that . . . boy, she has been looking for a way to contact reinforcements. And Parker nearly has what he is looking for."*

Gronk growled at the lizard woman. DeDe had never seen him act this way; he was always so gentle.

"Okay," DeDe said with uncertainty. "How do I stop Mr. Parker?"

"Get that book away from him. Destroy it if you can. He must not be allowed to find his word."

"His word? What the heck—"

"Go!"

Annoyed, DeDe closed her eyes and concentrated on the cave.

* * *

Back in the cave, Adam stood next to Mr. Parker, trying to engage the teacher.

DeDe stood and yelled to him, "Adam, get away! He's dangerous."

Adam gave her a strange look. "Dangerous? Look at him. How dangerous could he be? He just sits there reading that stupid book and yelling out random words."

"Gnintghil," said Mr. Parker.

Suddenly, the cave lit up, and Parker was engulfed in a bright crimson luminescence. There was a loud thunderous noise as the air exploded around him.

The powerful concussive force of the thunder knocked Adam across the room. He flew through the air like a rag doll. Instinctively, DeDe moved at SkySpeed to catch him. He landed unconscious in her arms, and she slowly lowered him to the cave floor and turned to her former English teacher.

The frail man she knew as Dennis Parker was gone. A large, red devil wearing a genie costume stood in his place. "I am free at last. I have found my magic word. I will have my revenge!" The twelve-foot-tall demon ranted, laughing maniacally.

DeDe thought about Boosadah's warning: "Beware his word." She bent down and picked up Adam to move him into the shadows at the opposite end of the cave. She laid the football player gently on the ground and turned toward the creature. The monster formerly known as Mr. Parker was still ignoring them.

DeDe quickly examined Adam. He was breathing normally and appeared to be okay. She picked up her backpack and moved deeper into the darkest corner of the cave.

The red demon had apparently finished his rant and remembered the students in the cave. The creature moved toward the unconscious football player. "And you, Mr. Berg, shall be the first to feel the wrath of Genie-Dman."

Before the monster could take another step, a large rock flew across the room and slammed into the devil, knocking him across the room.

"I knew it," the fully costumed Sky Girl announced as she floated from her hiding spot in the corner of the cave. "If I hung back and let you talk, you would eventually identify yourself. It works every time. Genie-Dman."

"Sky Girl!" the monster yelled and turned towards her. "I have been warned about you."

"Really? My reputation precedes me?" she asked as she landed halfway between Genie-Dman and Adam.

"I doubt you will be much of a problem."

"Oh, I'm not the problem." DeDe put her hands on her hips and spoke with determination. "I'm the solution."

The creature laughed.

Sky Girl stared at the creature. "I don't suppose you're ready to give up."

"Here is your answer," Genie-Dman's announced as he tackled her to the ground. Dust from the cave floor flew around them.

"Never been hit so hard," Sky Girl said in a dazed voice. She winced and tried to get her bearings, but the monster grabbed her red hair and pulled, easily throwing her across the room. She smashed into the rocks that blocked the entrance to the cave. The impact pulverized most of the rocks and knocked the rest away.

"You fool! I will destroy you for what your predecessor did to me. He and his cursed Protectorate hid my word!" The monster threw his body against the heroine in a wrestling body slam. "I will crush you, Sky Girl, and your vaunted Protectorate."

Sky Girl began to black out. She looked over at her unconscious friend. "I'm sorry, Adam. I tried," she said as she slumped to the ground. She could feel the monster's cold hands as Genie-Dman picked her up. Unable to stop him, she hung like a limp rag doll in his arms as his hands tightened around her neck.

The monster slowly raised her over his head. "I will smash you, little girl. You will pay for SkyBoy's crimes!"

Sky Girl could do nothing but listen to Dman's raving.

Then she heard another sound.

A loud roar filled the cave. The noise surprised Genie-Dman, causing the monster to drop Sky Girl, who rolled limply to the cave floor next to Adam. She struggled to lift her head to see what had made the noise.

Jason and another large creature stood in the entrance of a hidden passage in the cave. Sky Girl immediately recognized the creature from Jason's comic book; it was Jersey Devil.

141

"You!" Dman yelled.

"Us!" Jason replied smugly. He winked and smiled at Sky Girl. "My name is Jason Shewstal. I am here to rescue you."

"Dork," Sky Girl muttered weakly.

The Jersey Devil leapt into battle with the evil genie devil.

Jason ran over to Sky Girl and helped her up. "Seriously, DeDe, are you ok?"

"Mmm—okay. Just need to catch my breath." She strained to smile at him. "So I see you made a friend."

"Not just a friend—reinforcements," he said proudly.

"Ohmygosh, reinforcements! Miss Nitro!" Without hesitation, Sky Girl smashed through the cave wall and flew away.

Jason watched with a look of confusion as Sky Girl flew away. "I guess she was feeling better." He shrugged his shoulders and turned to watch the battle between Jersey Devil and Genie-Dman.

Large sparks flew each time the creatures clashed in battle. Jason sat on the ground and moved closer to Adam and checked on the unconscious football player. Once he was sure he was okay, Jason turned back to the battle. "Adam, you do not know what you are missing. This is better than any movie I have ever seen." After a moment, he pouted. "I wish I had some popcorn."

#

Outside, Miss Nitro had climbed to the top of a large hill. She examined the cell phone she held in her hand. "Finally!" she exclaimed. "I thought I would never get a signal out here."

She dialed a number and listened for the cell phone to connect. After the first ring, the phone began to smoke and spark. "What?" she exclaimed.

Sky Girl floated over the hill. "Sorry, Miss Nitro, you've gone over your monthly minutes, and now it's time to pay."

Miss Nitro gave her a condescending look.

"All right, I admit it. I almost winced at how corny that one sounded. I really need to work on this banter stuff."

Miss Nitro turned and reached for something on her belt. Before she could finish, Sky Girl easily scooped her up and tossed her into a water trough outside the cabin.

"That should prevent any more explosive surprises. Or maybe I should say, 'You're all wet, Nitro.' Give up." Sky Girl put her hands on her hips and assumed her heroic stance as the villain crawled out of the trough.

"Never!" Miss Nitro yelled and ran into the woods toward the cave. Sky Girl was about to follow when the cabin door began to open.

Nicole opened the door and emerged yawning from the cabin. "I could have sworn I heard someone out here." She looked around in confusion. "Adam? Are you out here?" After a moment, she turned around and yawned again. "Must have been a dream or something," she said as she went back inside to return to her nap.

If Nicole had only looked up, she would have seen Sky Girl floating upside down a mere three feet above her head. The superhero sighed. "That was close." She landed softly on the ground and turned to follow Miss Nitro.

As soon as she entered the woods, Sky Girl heard a loud scream followed by a roar from the cave. At SkySpeed, she rushed into the dark cave.

It took a moment for her eyes to adjust, but when they did, she found that both Miss Nitro and Genie-Dman had vanished. Jersey Devil stood in the center of the room, holding a smoking lamp triumphantly over his head. Jason stood next to the exhausted-looking creature, apparently trying to comfort him.

"Should I even ask?" Sky Girl said from the entrance.

"It was awesome!" Jason squeeled.

Jersey Devil turned to Sky Girl and spoke in a heavy English accent, "So Jason, young chap, are you going to introduce me to your young friend with the strange yet familiar taste in costuming?"

CHAPTER 25

Jason and DeDe, now dressed in her street clothes, stood next to a large bed, which held an unconscious Adam. The bed glowed with an eerie red light, reflecting off the sleeping boy's face. A moment later a computer printout shot out from one of the bed posts.

Jason watched with amazement at the diagnostic device.

DeDe didn't care about the device; she was focused on Adam. "Is he going to be okay?"

Jersey Devil ripped the printout from the post with a taloned finger. He adjusted his reading glasses and moved the printout closer to his face, reviewing the readouts in silence.

DeDe stared at him in anticipation. "So is he okay?" she repeated.

After a moment, Jersey Devil announced, "Your friend has bumped his head. He should be out for a few more hours, but he will be quite fine. A few minutes under the healing red light and I daresay he may even be better than before."

DeDe exhaled the breath she hadn't realized she'd been holding.

Jason smirked and put his hand on her shoulder. "See? He may even be better than before. As if you could believe that could ever be possible."

DeDe blushed.

"So," Jersey Devil said as he turned from the bed, "who wants tea? I'm brewing."

#

Twenty minutes later, Jason was finishing up his story as the trio sat around an ornate stone table drinking tea. "So I woke up in the cave and found Jersey Devil."

"Please, I told you to call me JD," he corrected.

"I found JD. I explained to him what had happened with you and Miss Nitro."

JD continued the story. "Yes, and once I found Jason, I immediately surmised that evil forces were at play. I brought him here to my secondary cave so I could consult with the Oracle. Luckily, I was able to trap Tina Nitro and Genie-D-man in Aladdin's magic lamp."

"Yes, that Aladdin," Jason interrupted. "Oh, and the Oracle is so cool. It lights up the whole room."

"Yes," JD continued, "and—"

"Tell her what it is made of," Jason said excitedly.

"Yes, I was—"

"You want to know?" Jason interrupted again. "You will never guess."

DeDe put her hand over his mouth and smiled. "Shhh, I don't want to hear it from the annoying geek. Let the scary monster tell the story."

JD harrumphed. "I prefer cryptozoological creature or urban legend. 'Scary Monster' is so uncivilized." He held up the tea pot. "More tea?"

"I heartily apologize. How dreadful I must sound," DeDe said in an attempt to copy his sophisticated tone. She held up her cup, and JD poured the tea. She still had her right hand over Jason's mouth.

"Shall I continue?" JD asked as his horse mouth curled into a smile.

"Please do."

"The oracle is made up of all the world's lost memories of SkyBoy," JD said as he sipped from his cup. Jason nodded emphatically under DeDe's hand, which still covered his mouth.

"Really?" DeDe squealed. "You know about what happened to my father?"

JD was confused. "Your father? Yes, of course I know what happened to your father."

"Tell me."

Jason grabbed his friend's hand as she began to rise into the air. "DeDe, you are floating away in excitement."

DeDe slowly sank back in the chair. "Sorry." She turned to JD. "What really happened to my father?"

JD gave her a strange look. "They didn't tell you? I assumed they would."

"Who?" DeDe asked. "Who would tell me what?"

"Why, the Protectorate of course. They are the ones who did it to him."

"I don't understand. What did the Protectorate do to SkyBoy?"

"Why, nothing."

DeDe was dumbstruck. "Now you're covering up for them?"

"JD, you are not making sense," Jason said, trying to help. "What happened to DeDe's father?"

Adam groaned from the bed, and JD looked over. "I'm afraid I've said too much, already. Your answers must come from the Protectorate." The creature stood up. "But now I must take my leave before your friend wakes up." He picked up the lamp. "I will ensure that these two remain trapped for some time. I believe a millennium or two may temper their evil tendencies."

"Please, tell me about my father," DeDe pleaded. A single tear fell down her cheek, and JD wiped it with a clawed talon.

"The tears of a child are a powerful currency." He took a deep breath. "Gronk. He is the key to unlocking the secret of your father."

DeDe was confused. "Gronk?"

"That is all I can say. I am truly sorry. I have to go," JD said and vanished in a flash of light, along with all the equipment in the room. Although a mere second ago they'd been in the middle of a high-tech laboratory, holding tea cups, Adam, Jason, and DeDe were left in the middle of a barren cave. Adam lay on the ground, still sleeping.

Jason took his friend's hand. "Do not worry, DeDe. We will figure out what happened."

DeDe clenched her hands into fists and stomped, suddenly furious. "Oh, I'm going to find out right now!" With determination, she closed her eyes and slumped in Jason's arms. He slowly moved her to the ground next to Adam.

Jason looked around the dark cave. "Sure, I will just sit back here and wait." Sounds of screeching that echoed throughout the cave. "Just me and the bats. Maybe I'll be inspired to strike fear into the cowardly and superstitious lot of criminals." Jason joked. But once he realized that no one was there to hear him, he felt silly.

* * *

DeDe opened her eyes in the Hall of the Protectorate.

Boosadah and three wolf guards were huddled in the front of the room. DeDe recognized a map of Colonia on an ornate metal table in front of them.

"We need to talk!" She insisted as she approached the group.

Boosadah did not look up. "Not now, child." She turned to the guards. "He could not have gotten far. Check the park and his old hideouts. Try to wound him if you can. But he must be brought back by any means necessary."

DeDe slammed her fist down on the table. It shattered the countertop in two. "We need to talk now!"

The wolf guards turned to her with their weapons drawn. Boosadah waved them away. "You have your orders. Go!"

They scampered away.

"Now, Deidre, what is so important that you must destroy my antique table? The civilization that created it no longer exists."

"Don't take that tone with me. Tell me about my father. I saw JD, and he said . . ." Tears began to stream down her face.

"That is—" Boosadah tried to find the right word. "—unfortunate."

"Unfortunate?" DeDe screeched. "What is so unfortunate?"

"Child, we will talk when the time is right, I promise." Boosadah moved to touch DeDe's shoulder, but DeDe shrugged her away.

"Get away." She took a breath and wiped the tears from her eyes, knowing she had to try a different tactic. "Where's Gronk?"

"He has escaped," Boosadah said sadly.

149

DeDe thought about the gentle rock creature and didn't understand. "Escaped? He was a prisoner?"

"It is not what you think."

"Where is he?" *She looked at the shattered map on the ground and remembered the wolf guards and their weapons.* "You are hunting for him in Colonia."

Boosadah was quiet for a moment. Finally she spoke. "Yes. The Protectorate believes he is too dangerous to roam free. They sent the wolf guards. But with your help—"

"With my help?" *DeDe yelled.* "I'm not going to help you hurt that poor creature!"

"Not hurt, find."

"No way!" *DeDe crossed her arms and turned away.*

Boosadah became annoyed and spoke sternly. "Must I remind you that you are an agent of this Protectorate? You work for us."

"Not anymore." *DeDe threw her hands up.* "I quit!"

Boosadah gasped, open-mouthed. "You cannot quit. Sky Girl is needed—especially now."

"Oh, I'll still be Sky Girl." *As DeDe began to vanish, she screamed,* "But, I quit the Protectorate! I quit the Council! And I quit you!"

CHAPTER 26

Later That Week

DeDe closed her locker. "Did you do the chemistry reading? I hope we don't have another pop quiz." She turned to Jason and pouted. "I think I liked it better when we had an evil chimp teaching us. Or even the evil demolitionist."

Jason did not respond.

DeDe turned to see what had caused her normally loquacious best friend to lull into an uncharacteristic silence.

Jason stared down the hall, lost in thought.

DeDe followed his gaze and immediately saw why he was completing ignoring her. Jason was staring at the object of his affection—Angela Leary.

The cute brunette was dressed in a Debole Academy cheerleading uniform. She stood at the far end of the hall, talking to her friends, and as usual, she had no idea Jason was staring.

"Oh, will you just go and talk to her?" DeDe whispered. "You've had a crush on her since the third grade."

Jason shook his head from side to side and stared.

DeDe's grin widened. "Don't say I never did anything for you, geek boy." The teen used her SkyStrength to nudge Jason down the hall. His sneakers scraped on the floor as the force of the blow forced him to slide directly into Angela's path. His sneakers squeaked as he tried to stop.

Angela's eyes widened at his appearance. "Hi Jason," she said with a smile.

Jason tried to catch his balance on the wall, acting like he was leaning on it nonchalantly. He lowered his voice and said, "Hey."

"Are you coming to the game tonight?" Angela asked with a demure smile.

Jason tried and failed to sound confident. "Oh, yeah. I will be there with you...at the game...um, not with you, but in the stands...you know. Um, cool." The bell rang, saving him from himself. "I, uh, better go. We have chemistry. Uh, I have to go to chemistry." He turned and ran into the classroom. But not before accidentally walking into a freshman and knocking the underclassman's books to the floor.

DeDe was already in her chair. She watched as her best friend awkwardly piled the books into the freshman's arms and slowly lumbered into his seat. When Jason was settled, DeDe turned to him and lowered her voice in a goofy impression. "Duh, oh, yeah. I will be there with you...at the game...um, not with you, but in the stands, you know. Um, cool.' Duh!"

She opened her book and smirked. "That's it. You don't get to criticize my banter anymore."

Jason turned crimson. He touched the rubber soul of his sneaker; it was still warm. "I think you melted my favorite pair of sneakers."

DeDe snorted.

"This day cannot get any worse," Jason mumbled.

Professor Katinsky, the substitute chemistry teacher, walked into the room. "Books closed. It's time for another surprise quiz."

Jason put his head on the desk and mumbled into the wood, "I miss Commander Chimp."

CHAPTER 27

An hour later, Jason and DeDe sat in the cafeteria as Jason continued to whine about the surprise chemistry test. He flipped through a *Legendary Heroes of Myth* comic book as he pushed away the red plastic tray with green Jell-O on it. The gelatinous mass shimmied with the movement. "I am so depressed; I cannot even enjoy my *Mulan* story."

"Poor baby. I have something that will cheer you up," DeDe said as she reached for her purple backpack under the table. "I need help with a new search patrol to find Gronk." She unzipped her backpack and took out a map of Middlesex County. She had used highlighters and colored pens to draw large circles on the map.

"I looked over by Merrill Park last night. So tonight, after the game, I guess I'll look over the area by JFK High School." DeDe pointed to the school on the map.

Jason nodded.

DeDe gave him a curious look. "Um, this is the part where you give me your anti-football, superhero priority lecture."

Jason laughed. "No lecture today. I think that sounds great. Bring your costume and I will grab the extra set of wireless earpieces. We can meet and walk over together before kickoff and search for Gronk after the game."

DeDe gave him a funny look. "Who are you? And what have you done with Jason Shewstal?"

Then DeDe remembered Angela's cheerleading uniform. DeDe gave Jason a knowing smile as she put the map away. "I guess we can go stare at Angela for a while first."

Jason nodded before he processed DeDe's words. "Right, and then— Hey!"

The lunch bell rang, interrupting Jason's rant, and they packed up their bags and started up the stairs toward their lockers.

As they walked through the crowded halls, DeDe whispered, "I sure hope we find Gronk. I'm not even sure he's in Colonia, but that's what Boosadah thought." She opened her locker and turned to Jason, who had done the same, "I still can't believe the Protectorate treated him that way."

"I still cannot believe you quit over it," Jason said as he opened his bag, took out the *Official Handbook of the SkyBoy Universe,* and shoved it into his locker. "And they had such cool toys." Jason removed a pair of micro-tech earpieces from the locker and shoved them into his pocket. "Given how quickly we are going through these things lately, we may have to go back to the headsets soon."

"I hate those headsets," DeDe whined. "They get caught in my mask and hair." DeDe shivered at the thought. "Let's talk about something else."

The Sky Girl conversation over, Jason resumed whining about Mr. Katinsky's test.

CHAPTER 28

Bright lights illuminated the football field of the Debole Academy. Despite the brisk fall night, tickets had completely sold out and the stands were packed with students, alumni, and parents dressed in the Debole Academy's burgundy and grey school colors. School spirit spread through the stand in the form of half-finished cheers and band music that drifted through the air and mixed with the smell of various food concessions.

Jason and DeDe sat in their usual seats in the front row of the bleachers. Jason rubbed his hands together and zipped up his winter jacket, concealing the *Real Vampires Don't Sparkle* sweatshirt underneath. He looked over at DeDe, who wore jeans and a thin, black, long-sleeved *Phantom of the Opera* shirt.

"You know, you could at least act like the cold bothers you."

DeDe put her arm around her friend. "Poor baby. We'll get you a hot chocolate during halftime."

Jason mumbled something about marshmallows and turned to watch the game. The Debole Academy football team was

157

doing extremely well, and thanks in large part to Adam's excellent quarterbacking, the game was rapidly becoming a blowout. Not for the first time tonight, he turned his attention to the sideline.

DeDe leaned forward as she watched Adam score yet another first down. "Check out Adam's moves. He's on fire tonight. I think the Debole Academy is on its way to another state championship."

"Hard to believe he is even able to play after what happened in the cave. I guess JD's healing ray really did make him better than ever," Jason said as his eyes scanned the sideline.

In the week since the cave incident, Adam had paid more attention to her—a lot more. He had called her pretty much every night. The two had talked for hours and hours. As a result, they had grown much closer. Adam confessed his fears that he would let the team down. DeDe understood more than he could know.

Adam and DeDe were still just friends, but for the first time, DeDe thought there could actually be a chance for more.

"DeDe! You are doing it again!" Jason chastised as he grabbed her shoulder and pushed her down.

The teen realized that she was floating up from her seat and forced herself back down to the bleacher. Floating was a bad habit she had developed since the cave-in. In fact, Jason had had to remind her to stop floating and stay on the ground several times during the past week.

The crowd roared as Adam scored another touchdown. The quarterback looked triumphantly at the crowd and directly at DeDe. He smiled and pointed at her. She blushed and waved shyly in return. "Did you see that?" she whispered.

Jason ignored her. The lanky teen was too busy staring at Angela and the other cheerleaders to notice the game. DeDe followed his gaze and saw Nicole, in her cheerleading uniform, glaring at her. "Well, I guess somebody saw it."

Their eyes met, and the two girls stared at each other, neither looking away in their battle of wills. DeDe knew she was being petty, but she didn't really care.

She hated Nicole.

Suddenly, DeDe heard a strange sound. Focusing her SkyHearing to locate the source of the noise, she identified the source of the sound. It was coming from behind the bleachers.

DeDe hated to concede the staring match with her rival. She sighed as she turned away to use her SkyVision to see the problem.

Through the darkness, DeDe saw three men with large guns just outside the ticket booth. She heard the strange noise again as the villain's cocked their pistols. Inside the ticket booth, a fourth figure, a girl, was putting the receipts into a safe. DeDe leaned over to Jason and grabbed his arm. "We have to go."

"But the game is not over," he said with a whine as he stared at the cheerleader pyramid that had formed with Nicole and Angela on top.

DeDe pinched his arm.

"Owww! Why did you do that?"

She made eye contact and spoke in a very deliberate tone. "I said we have to go. I lost my contact lens, and I need your help to find it," DeDe said, using the secret code signal they had developed the previous year during MechApe's attack.

"Oh. Your contact," he said as he stood up and grabbed her backpack. "I get it. What are we waiting for? Come on!"

The pair politely pushed their way to the end of the bleachers and rushed out of the stands, then ran around to the back and stood under the bleachers. Jason stood watch with his back to her as DeDe changed into her uniform at SkySpeed.

A second later, DeDe was gone, replaced by Sky Girl, dressed in her black and purple costume. Sky Girl handed Jason DeDe's backpack as he passed her the small earpiece.

"What is the problem?" Jason asked.

"I think somebody is robbing the box office," she said, placing the wireless earpiece in her right ear.

"Well, that should not take long," he said as he put his own earpiece in. "We can still catch the end of the game." But Sky Girl was gone.

"Let's hope you're right," she said in her deeper Sky Girl voice over his earpiece.

#

On the other side of the field, three figures dressed in garish costumes brandished large six-shooters as they entered the box office. The leader aimed his weapon at the young woman who was dressed in a pin-striped concession uniform, working in the office.

"You'se better open the safe!" the man commanded in a heavy Brooklyn accent.

"I can't!" the teenager cried. "It's sealed electronically with a time lock!"

The leader huffed in disgust. "Move it or lose it, girlie." He stepped in front of the large wall safe and issued orders to his two henchmen. "Klapon, tie her up. Klapuf, guard the door." They did as he ordered. Klapon wrapped the teen in thick ropes and forced her to sit on the floor.

The leader put his gun away and removed his gloves, revealing his glowing hands. The girl gasped as the man smacked his hands together in the direction of the safe and large shockwave emitted from the impact. The blast shorted out the lock in the safe and the door swung slowly open.

"Cool beans!" the villain exclaimed. "It looks like dis school made lots of money on da game. Klapuf, get over here."

There was a noise at the door, followed by the sounds of a punch and a male grunt.

"Wha—?" said the leader.

A second later, an unconscious Klapuf slid across the floor.

All eyes turned to the door.

Sky Girl stood in the doorway and pointed at the leader. "The only money you'll be getting is prison minimum wage." She tried not to wince when she heard Jason groan over the cheesy line through her earpiece.

"Sky Girl! Abouts time you got here. Feel my power!"

Sky Girl tried not to show her surprise. This was the second villain who'd known of her costumed identity. Instead, she placed her hands on her hips and said, "I don't know who you are, but I'm here to stop you."

Taking the cue, Jason spoke to Sky Girl through the earpiece. "He said, 'Feel my power.' We need to figure out who he is and what powers he has. What is he wearing?"

"You five-foot, ten-inch, black-costumed man with gold lightning bolts and a blue face mask—uh—guy."

The ticket salesgirl rolled her eyes. Sky Girl immediately recognized her as Jennifer Holton from gym class. Sky Girl assumed that if the costume hadn't done the job, that last outburst would have convinced Jennifer that she was crazy.

At least Sky Girl had provided enough information for Jason to figure out whom she faced. "His name is Klapper. He has the ability to short electrical systems and, uh, other thingies."

"Did you just dumb down the villain for me?" Sky Girl asked in a resentful whisper.

"I will destroy you! My power is fierce," Klapper said menacingly.

"Really?" Sky Girl said in disbelief. "With a name like Klapper?"

"Really!" Klapper and Jason said at the same time.

"The game is almost over," Jason added. "You need to end this now, before it gets too crowded."

As if on cue, Sky Girl heard the buzzer that signaled the end of the fourth quarter and the game. Taking advantage of her momentary distraction, Klapon attacked. He tried to hit her with a metal crowbar from behind, but the metal object simply vibrated with the impact.

Sky Girl turned to him. "Bad vibrations?"

"Classic line!" Jason said over the earpiece.

Sky Girl smiled as she grabbed the crowbar from Klapon and wrapped the thick metal bar around his wrists. She picked the henchman up and threw him against the concrete wall. The thug slammed against the wall with a thud and slid down it slowly. He was unconscious by the time he landed on the floor.

Sky Girl turned to Klapper. "Who's next?"

\#

The crowd was starting to exit the football field. To avoid discovery, Jason snuck into the school cafeteria. The large room was dark except for the lights coming from under the locker room doors and the red exit signs that reflected off the cafeteria tables.

Jason looked toward the locker room. He knew the football team and cheerleaders, including Angela, were changing. He thought about how he had almost witnessed that event the previous year before Commander Chimp had intervened. Jason forced the thoughts out of his head and double-checked to make sure he was alone in the cafeteria. "Just make sure he does not clap his hands," he whispered into his headset. "Keep them apart."

#

Back in the ticket booth, Sky Girl failed to hear Jason clearly. Before she could ask him to repeat himself, Klapper slammed his glowing hands together with a large, smacking noise. Waves of concussive force emitted from the villain's hands and slammed into Sky Girl, throwing her against the wall where she had just thrown Klapon. The impact knocked the wind from her.

"Okay, that hurt." She winced as she got to her feet, touched her earpiece, and whispered, "Hey, Jason, how do I beat this guy?" The only response she heard was static. "That's just great. I'm on my own," Sky Girl mumbled as she turned back to Klapper.

#

Jason grabbed his ear and pulled out his earpiece as high-pitched feedback echoed through the device. He quickly put the earpiece back in and activated the device. "Sky Girl!" he yelled. "Sky Girl! Are you there?" There was only static. "The connection is dead—I need to get to the box office and help." As Jason turned to exit the cafeteria, he heard a scream come from the girls' locker room. He recognized the voice immediately as Angela Leary's. Jason dropped DeDe's backpack on a table near the door and ran toward the source of the screaming, knowing his best friend could handle herself. "I guess DeDe is on her own. I just hope she finishes up in time to rescue me."

#

Sky Girl's body slammed against the ticket booth wall again.

"A fellow could get used to this," Klapper said on a laugh.

Sky Girl looked up at him with bleary eyes. The villain spoke into an earpiece that looked remarkably similar to hers. She wondered how a villain had gotten access to a Protectorate communications device.

One thing was clear. "I'm getting a little tired of hitting the wall," Sky Girl said as she stood up and faced him.

"Copy that" Klapper whispered into his earpiece and turned toward the heroine. "Welp, Sky Girl, I gots to go. See ya, babe. It's been fun. Well, fun for me, at least." He laughed and pressed a button on his watch. A strange glow engulfed the trio, and Klapper and his two unconscious henchmen began to disappear.

Before they had completely vanished, Sky Girl used her SkySpeed to snatch the money bag from Klapper's grip. She sighed as the villain disappeared. "Well, at least you failed to rob the ticket booth."

Klapper laughed. "You assume I was here for the money. Babe, I was the diversion." The villain vanished, leaving Sky Girl alone with Jennifer Holton.

"Diversion? For what?" a confused Sky Girl wondered as she used her SkyStrength to free Jennifer from the ropes that bound the concession's attendant.

She had a lot of questions for Jason.

Jennifer rubbed her wrists. "I can't believe it. You were amazing," she said in awe.

Sky Girl blushed. "Jenny, I'm just glad you're okay."

"Yeah, I'm fine." She stared up at her rescuer with a curious look. "Hey, how do you know my name?"

Sky Girl blushed a brighter color of red as she realized her mistake. She was secretly glad that she had broken her ear piece; Jason never would have let her hear the end of this. "It's, um, on your name badge." The heroine turned to the door and flew off as quickly as she could.

A second later, Jennifer Holton realized she wasn't wearing a name badge.

CHAPTER 29

Sky Girl flew high above the Debole Academy. She could see the lights on the football field and the tiny dots that were walking toward the parking lot.

Flashing red and blue lights appeared outside of the cafeteria.

"Police cars? An ambulance!" Sky Girl observed as she flew down until she was only a few feet above the building. She peered down at the cafeteria with her SkyVision to examine the scene. The walls and ceiling of the school vanished and were replaced by several pink and blue images. She could see various emergency personnel moving around the area near the locker rooms. She could also see the heat signature of several men tending to victims inside the locker room. She focused her SkyHearing and tried to eavesdrop on the men.

"Are they all like this?" the first one asked as he examined a prone body.

"Yeah. There's nothing wrong with them. They just won't wake up," the second confirmed.

Sky Girl landed on the patio outside the door of the cafeteria and peered in through the small glass window on the door. Her purple backpack with her street clothes was lying on a table right where Jason had left them. At SkySpeed, she flew in, scooped up her pack, and quickly changed as she moved toward the locker room. A breeze blew through the cafeteria, rustling napkins and disturbing posters on the wall.

Sky Girl listened as she changed. She focused on every detail since she knew Jason would want a complete report when they compared notes later.

"What's the story with this one? All these girl cheerleaders and one guy?" the first EMT asked.

DeDe inhaled sharply. She had a sinking feeling in the pit of her stomach.

"I found his school identification card," the second EMT announced.

DeDe hoped her fears would not be affirmed as she put her hand on the closed door.

"It says his name is—"

DeDe held her breath.

"—Jason Shewstal."

DeDe pushed her way in through the door, which nearly came off its hinges. "Jason!" She exclaimed.

"I thought you locked that door," the EMT said as he moved to stop DeDe, but she easily pushed him aside.

DeDe kneeled by her best friend and cradled his head. Jason's skin was pale, and there was a neutral expression on his face. His breathing was shallow. "What happened?" she choked.

Several EMTs tried to grab DeDe's arms, but she would not budge. Finally, they gave up trying to move her. One of them put a hand on her shoulder and lowered his voice to a soft whisper, "Miss, please. I know you're concerned. Please let us do our job."

DeDe nodded, put Jason's head down, and moved to the side. "Who did this?" she again asked, this time with a more adamant tone to her voice.

"We don't know," the EMT admitted as he tended to Jason. "Maybe no one." He stood up and turned to DeDe. "I have never seen anything like it. Every cheerleader and your friend have the same symptoms. There is nothing physically wrong with them. It could be viral. We won't know until the CDC gets here."

DeDe glanced around the locker room.

For the first time she noticed that all of the girls from the cheerleading squad were also in the locker room. Still in their uniforms, they were all in the same condition as Jason, scattered around the locker room. They appeared to have simply collapsed where they'd been standing, some near the shower, others near the lockers. Angela Leary had a look of fear on her half made-up face as she lay next to her scattered makeup kit.

Ignoring everything around her, DeDe moved to the corner of the locker room and sat cross-legged on a bench. She closed her eyes and centered herself, exhaling slowly.

* * *

DeDe opened her eyes.

But nothing happened.

She had expected to end up in the Hall of the Galactic Protectorate. She closed her eyes and tried again.

* * *

Again, when she opened her eyes, nothing happened.

"I have to do something." She sighed as she closed her eyes again and began to focus. This time, DeDe used her SkyHearing to listen to her surroundings. She could hear the EMTs as they examined Jason and the cheerleaders; she could hear Jason's faint heartbeat and tried to ignore her best friend's fragile condition.

She then focused outward. Adam and the other football players celebrated their victory in the other locker room, unaware of what was happening in the room next to them.

DeDe slowly exhaled in relief that Adam was safe.

Sensing no problem in the boy's locker room, DeDe moved her senses further out. She listened to the conversations of the fans on their way to the parking lot. She could almost taste the exhaust from the cars as some of the older students and the parents drove out of the parking lot onto Tingley Lane.

Sweat began to form on her brow as she tried to listen for something—anything—unusual.

There was nothing.

DeDe gave up and opened her eyes. A piece of matted red hair fell from her forehead and into her eyes. She blew the hair out of her face and stood up. Then she heard something— slow, nervous breathing. "I was focusing too far away," she murmured.

DeDe closed her eyes and focused her SkyHearing again.

The sound was coming from somewhere inside the room.

"You guys better get ready," DeDe said to the paramedics as she opened her eyes and stood up.

She moved slowly in the direction of the sound—toward the row of large standing lockers. DeDe remembered that Jason had hid in one of these standing lockers to spy on Commander

Chimp last year. Someone else was doing the same thing now and spying on them.

DeDe approached a group of three lockers and stood in front of them and listened intently. The breathing was clearly coming from the middle locker. She reached for the handle and yanked, but it was locked. Using her SkyStrength, she tried to gently force the lock. Instead, the entire locker door ripped off its hinges in her hand. She smiled shyly as she said, "Oops. It must have been broken."

The EMTs nodded in confusion as they took the heavy locker door from her.

Two EMTs struggled to carry the door to the corner of the room.

DeDe peered into the locker and saw a girl dressed in a cheerleader's uniform. The cheerleader sat crouched in the fetal position, facing the back of the locker and rocking back and forth slowly. The girl was breathing heavily and shaking. She turned her head slowly.

"Nicole!" DeDe exclaimed as she recognized the locker's lone occupant. She reached into the locker to help Nicole out.

Reluctant at first, Nicole took DeDe's hand and climbed out of the dark locker. Nicole's arrogant swagger had been replaced by a look of dazed confusion. Tears streamed down the older girl's face. Mascara ran down her cheeks in black streaks.

"It was horrible." She sobbed as she clutched DeDe's hand.

"What was horrible?" DeDe asked as Nicole gripped her hand tighter. Surprisingly, DeDe could feel the pressure despite her SkyInvulnerability.

Nicole looked directly into DeDe's eyes. "The locker room went dark, then . . . there were black robes. And that voice...that horrible voice."

Nicole screamed and then passed out. DeDe caught the cheerleader's limp body before it could hit the floor.

She held Nicole for a few seconds before the stunned EMTs were able to react and take the cheerleader. They immediately began to treat the unconscious Nicole.

DeDe stepped away and let the paramedics do their work. She moved closer to Jason's unconscious body. She took his hand and tried to hold back the tears. It was obvious that she couldn't go to the Protectorate for help—they were unavailable to her.

Finally, she lost control. Tears rolled down DeDe's cheeks. "How am I going to do this without you?" she choked.

This time, Sky Girl was truly on her own.

CHAPTER 30

Hours later, DeDe still sat in the hospital waiting room. She had been there since they'd brought Jason and the girls in for treatment. On the way to the hospital, DeDe had stopped by Jason's locker and retrieved his copy of *The Official Handbook of the SkyBoy Universe*. She had gently taken the book out of the Mylar bag and removed it from the white acetate backing board, and it now sat on her lap. DeDe flipped through the issue again.

The book was filled with listings for Commander Chimp, whom she knew, a dark doppelgänger known as Yobyks, a multi-page listing for Professor Z and his partner Evil Brain, and even half a page on Klapper. She read it again, but still could not find anything about him that would explain what had happened to Jason or the cheerleaders.

DeDe put the book aside and turned to look at the blank wall beside her. Not for the first time, she considered using her SkyVision to find out what was going on with Jason. DeDe looked at the sign banning the use of cell phones and thought better of it. She remembered what had happened to Miss

Backerchase's computer last year when she had accidentally SkyPulsed it. And while she clearly believed that she had developed better control over her abilities over the summer, she did not think a hospital was the best place to test that theory.

DeDe turned back to waiting room area. Adam sat across from her, still in his football pants and a white t-shirt. DeDe brushed the hair out of her face. "I'm sure Nicole will be fine," she said, trying to sound reassuring. "She wasn't like those other girls . . . or Jason. She was just shaken up."

Adam moved closer. "Thanks," he said looking down at the ground. "I'm sure your boyfriend is fine, too."

"What?" DeDe said in surprise.

"Your boyfriend. Jason."

She couldn't speak; she just stared at Adam in confusion.

He blushed. "Well, the way you talk about him all the time, I thought . . ."

DeDe's mouth dropped open. "Jason isn't my boyfriend. He's just . . ." Before DeDe could find the right word to describe her relationship with Jason, Adam spoke up.

"Really?" Adam asked with a note of excitement in his voice. "I mean, uh, that's . . ."

"DeDe!" a woman's voice called out. She looked up to see her mother, Dianne, rush in followed by her boyfriend, Michael Valjorge. "Thank goodness you're okay," she said, hugging her daughter. "I was so worried!"

DeDe hugged her back and spoke through gritted teeth, "Mom, you're embarrassing me in front of Adam."

Adam gave DeDe an uncomfortable smile when he caught her eye. DeDe returned the smile.

She moved away from her mother and blushed. "I'm fine. I'm here for Jason." Her voice cracked a bit. "Something's happened to him."

For the first time, DeDe saw the woman in the doorway: Doris Shewstal. The five-foot-tall stocky woman wore a grey muumuu. Heavy mascara dripped down her face, making her appear more like a raccoon than a woman.

"She cried all the way here," Dianne whispered.

"What's wrong with my baby?" Doris sobbed.

"I...I don't know," DeDe said with depressing honesty. "We're waiting for the doctor." She was afraid saying more would reveal her secret.

The door to the emergency room swung open, and Nicole was wheeled into the room by an orderly. Behind them walked an older man with a grey mustache and a long, burgundy overcoat. He nervously jingled the set of keys in his hand as he made his way across the room.

Adam stood up. "Hey, Nicole. Hello, Judge Debis."

DeDe gave Nicole a reassuring smile. "Are you okay? You looked a little shaky there in the locker."

"Shaky?" Nicole snapped. "I have no idea what you're talking about. You're lucky I don't sue you."

DeDe's brow creased in confusion and hurt. "But the man in the cloak—with the voice?"

Nicole gave her father a long look before turning back to DeDe. "What are you babbling about, you weirdo?" She threw her hands up. "Daddy, take me home."

Judge Debis pushed his daughter toward the exit. Adam's eyes met DeDe's, and he gave her a sad look. She thought he was about to say something. Instead, he turned away and followed Nicole and her father.

The doctor came out to talk Mrs. Shewstal shortly after. Since they were in the lobby and not near any equipment, DeDe risked using her SkyHearing to eavesdrop on the conversation. She picked up the copy of the SkyBoy handbook and pretended to read it.

"I don't understand," Doris said in a weak voice. "What is wrong with my boy?"

The doctor sighed. "We just don't know. His vitals are fine—all their vitals are fine. It's almost like he has no will to wake up. Like his spirit is gone."

"Please help him," Doris begged as she began to cry again.

"There has to be something we can do!" DeDe exclaimed as she threw Jason's SkyBoy handbook, along with the bag and board, onto the emergency room floor. An envelope fell out from behind the acetate board.

Michael picked up the book and envelope. He read the title of the book and chuckled as if he were in on a private joke. "You know," he said softly as he handed them back to DeDe, "when Jason gets better, he's going to want that back. And you know how he is about his books."

DeDe smiled. "Yeah, it's bad enough I took it out of its little baggie. Thanks, Mr. Valjorge."

"DeDe, you don't have to call me Mr. Valjorge. Your mom and I are getting closer, and we may be taking a very big step soon."

DeDe held her breath. Here it came. The moment she had feared.

"You can call me Michael or Mike."

DeDe exhaled and smiled, her relief apparent.

Michael chuckled at her reaction. "What? Did you think I was going to say dad? I care about you and your mother very

176

much, but I am not here to replace your father." He looked at the book in her hands. "Good golly. That's a battle even SkyBoy couldn't win."

DeDe was surprised at how much she was touched by his honesty. "thanks Mr.—Mike." She could feel the tears forming, so she quickly looked down and saw the envelope. It was addressed to "Sky Girl."

"What's that word on the envelope?" Michael asked, apparently spotting it at the same moment she had.

"Um, nothing. I've, uh, I've got to go." DeDe stuffed the envelope into her back pocket, scooped up her backpack, and rushed around the corner and into the ladies restroom.

She looked under all the stall doors to make sure no one else was there, then went to lock the door, but there was no latch. Using her SkyStrength, she bent the doorknob to keep anyone from getting in. Satisfied that she was alone, DeDe ducked into a stall, locked the door, and floated cross-legged a few feet above the floor. She didn't want to be disturbed.

The rays of the rising sun shone through a small window and reflected on the ceiling to illuminate the bathroom. With a shaky hand, DeDe ripped open the envelope. It contained two items: a letter and a map from the Internet with a printout of directions from Colonia to someplace in Reading, Pennsylvania.

The letter read:

Sky Girl,

If you are reading this, something has gone wrong and I cannot help you. I have enclosed directions to a secret location in central Pennsylvania. I hope these guys can help. Although they do not know your secret, they know more about SkyBoy than anyone on the planet, including me.

You are my hero.
Sidekicklad

DeDe's eyes began to tear up again, and she had trouble finishing the letter. She sobbed. "I have to find a way to help Jason. But how?"

"Sidekicklad?" She asked, looking at the signature on the letter. Why would Jason sign it in such a strange way? She read it again and examined the printed directions and map.

"I guess Sky Girl is going to Reading, Pennsylvania," DeDe said as she took her black and purple costume out of her backpack.

CHAPTER 31

Sky Girl flew high above the interstate, following the directions on the printout as best as she could while trying to stay out of sight of the cars below. She had still managed to get lost more than a few times.

It was early evening before she arrived at the address on the printout. Sky Girl landed and looked up at the sign on the building. Large neon letters identified it as Jamie's Comic Nest.

After making sure no one was around, Sky Girl quickly changed out of her costume and back into her street clothes behind a bush in front of the store.

A moment later, DeDe Christopher walked through the front door of Jamie's Comic Nest carrying her purple backpack.

"Can I help you?" a middle-aged blonde man asked from behind the counter. His name badge identified him as Jamie, the owner of the Comic's Nest.

"Uh, yeah," DeDe said as she approached the front of the counter. She was overwhelmed by the sheer number of comics in the store. She cleared her throat. "I was looking for something for my friend, Jason. He sent me here to get it."

Jamie thought for a moment. "I don't think I know a Jason. How would I know him?"

Jason had clearly sent her there. *Why would he do so if they didn't even know him?* she wondered. It was then that she remembered the weird signature.

"Sidekidlad," she said softly, trying not to sound silly. "Does that sound familiar?"

Jamie's eyes lit up. "Sidekicklad? I know Sidekicklad. He's on the forum. He's the big SkyBoy fan, right? "

"That's right," DeDe said hopefully. "Well, I was hoping, um, that . . ." DeDe paused, not knowing how to ask for help without giving herself up. She chastised herself for not thinking it through more carefully.

Two other men entered the store then. The first was a man with dark complexion and jet black hair. The second a paler, thinner man, had curly blonde hair and muttonchops. Jamie gave them a friendly wave. "Hello, my fellow geeks. I'm glad you're here. This is a friend of Sidekicklad. She had a question for me."

The darker man smiled. "Is this about that game he's working on?"

"Yeah," the other man interjected. "I thought I was a fan, but imagine—a game featuring all the enemies and allies of the whole SkyBoy Universe."

DeDe smiled at Jason's ingenuity. He could get all the information he needed online without anyone suspecting the truth—not that anyone would believe him anyway. "That's right. I wanted to surprise him with a special comic, but I can't remember the villain's name." She pouted and tried to look helpless.

Jamie's eyes lit up, and he pointed to the two men. "Well, Murd and Peter here know more about SkyBoy than I do, so they might know the character. I might have the book. We'd do anything for Sidekicklad."

Murd, the thinner man spoke. "I shall do my best not to be muddled."

The black-haired Peter added, "Go ahead and quiz me. I'm unstumpable."

"Too bad Bryan and Pants are on vacation again," Jamie added.

Peter laughed. "Please. Pants only knows about the Flash, and Bryan never remembers anything."

Murd gave DeDe a shy smile. "That would be an inside joke. Go ahead. Tell us your story."

DeDe took a deep breath and told them everything she knew. She mentioned Klapper and the man in the cloak with the voice and the eyes. She told them about what had happened to the cheerleaders.

She decided to conveniently leave out the involvement of Sky Girl and the fact that it had actually happened.

The three men thought for a moment. Finally, Peter said, "I don't think that ever happened. Not in any book I have ever seen." Seeing DeDe's sad reaction, he added, "But it sure sounds like the guy in the cloak is Shadow. I don't remember him ever working with Klapper, though."

"And while I don't think Shadow used the device," added Murd, "I believe the effects that you are describing could be caused by exposure to the Orb of Anacostium."

DeDe began to realize that Jason's faith in these guys was well placed. "The orb of ana...ana..."

"Orb of Anacostium," said Murd. "It was used by the Magum to resurrect his true love in SkyBoy Annual Thirteen. Apparently, Magum needed to gather a team of beloved people; it was the boy band in the story, if you can believe it. The orb swallowed their souls and put them in a deathlike trance. This generated a significant amount of energy—enough for Magum to perform the spell."

"Would a whole team of cheerleaders count as a beloved team?" DeDe asked.

Jamie piped up. "High school cheerleaders were certainly beloved by me."

Murd ignored Jamie and continued. "That would do it. The user of the orb could use the energy to do whatever they wanted or raise whomever he or she needed, and then, in your example, the cheerleaders would never wake up."

DeDe's voice was soft but stern. "How do I stop it?"

The three men stared at her.

She coughed. "I mean, in the game, how should SkyBoy stop this orb and save the cheerleaders?"

"Well," Murd said after a pause, "in the Annual, SkyBoy shattered the globe before the soul of the final group member could be collected. This returned all the other souls to their rightful bodies."

"I knew I had it!" Jamie interrupted, taking something down from the wall. "It was even signed by the author before he died." He handed DeDe SkyBoy Annual Number 13.

DeDe looked at the book and thought of her father, who had written it. She slowly ran her finger over the signature, hoping to feel a connection. She looked up at Murd. "And the Shadow?"

"Just Shadow." Peter chuckled. "No 'the.' That's someone else."

"Someone who knows the evil that lurks in the heart of man," Murd added in a deep radio voice.

"Okay, I get it. Just Shadow. So how do you beat him?" DeDe asked hopefully.

"As with any other shadow, a single candle can dispel the darkness," Murd responded somewhat philosophically.

DeDe stared at him in confusion.

"He can be beaten by shining a bright light on him," Murd explained. "But you would need to stop him before he gets all the cheerleaders. Otherwise he would be too powerful"

DeDe gasped "It's Nicole. She's the last cheerleader. I have to go!"

DeDe hugged all three men and moved to the door. "Thanks a lot, guys. You're wonderful." She scooped up her backpack and rushed out of the comic shop.

"Anytime," Peter said as DeDe walked out.

Jamie looked at the book on the counter. "I wanted to give her this for Sidekicklad. Murd, see if you can catch her."

Murd opened the door and looked out into the parking lot, but the girl had vanished. "I guess she had a ride," he said.

If Murd had looked up, he would have seen the girl, now dressed in black spandex, purple boots and gloves, and a long, flowing purple cape flying through the air.

Sky Girl raced through the evening sky back to Colonia at SkySpeed.

She only hoped she would be in time.

CHAPTER 32

The New Dover Road estate area lay on the outskirts of the main town of Colonia. The street consisted of expensive houses, each built on a large plot of property. Approximately every ten feet, a street light illuminated the manicured lawns and perfectly sculpted landscaping of each house.

The Debis mansion, Nicole's house, sat in the middle of New Dover Road and was the centerpiece of the neighborhood.

There was a soft popping noise as Klapper and his two henchmen appeared on the far end of the street.

Klapper turned and addressed Klapon and Klapuf, his henchmen. "Remember, we only want to kill the lights. We don't want no nosey neighbors out here because you'se dummies took out the power for the whole neighborhood."

With slow, deliberate purpose, Klapper approached the first street light. He clapped his hands together and sent a pulse wave that shorted out the bulb. He then moved on to each of the remaining lampposts on the street. One by one the lights went out. Soon New Dover Road was engulfed in total darkness. The only illumination visible was a flashing red bulb on the round transformer box that provided power to the entire neighborhood.

The villainous trio looked at their handiwork. Klapper smiled. "Okay, it's time for the next part of the plan."

The villains slowly made their way to house number 9102 and stood on the porch. The leader looked up and down New Dover Road to make sure no one was out on the street. Satisfied, he spoke into the radio. "Okay, boss. All da lights are out. You're all clear."

"Excellent!" an otherworldly voice responded. "Go into the house and prepare her for my arrival."

Klapon was clearly discomfited by the voice. "What about alarms? I bet all these expensive houses got them in spades."

Klapuf smacked him in the head. "You don't think the boss thought of that?"

Klapper smiled. "Yes, we got a man on the inside. He turned off the alarm."

Meanwhile, inside 9102 New Dover Road, Nicole Debis sat on her four-poster bed and spoke into a fire engine red telephone receiver. "No, Adam. I'm fine. I don't understand why you can't come over."

"I don't think—" Adam's voice responded over the phone.

"Oh, come on. Daddy's in his study. He'll never even know you're here, You know you love me," she added in a pouty voice.

Adam paused. "Listen, we need to talk about—"

Suddenly, the phone went dead.

"Adam?" Nicole asked, annoyed. Did Adam dare hang up on her?

Her annoyance turned to fear a second later when the lights went out in her room, leaving her in the dark.

"This is just like what happened in the locker room!" she gasped as she ran out of her room.

"Daddy?" Nicole yelled as she raced down the stairs into the living room.

She saw the figure in the darkness and called to him. "Daddy, I'm scared."

"Sorry, toots, Daddy ain't here. He's taking one for the team," the figure said in the darkness.

Nicole squinted and could just make out two other figures moving toward her.

She turned to run out of the living room, but the two henchmen blocked her way.

"Klapon! Klapuf! Get her!"

The henchmen reached out and grabbed Nicole tightly by the arms. She struggled, but the muscular henchmen held her firm.

"Let go!" she cried.

The two men dragged her toward the door like a rag doll. With a last burst of strength, she pushed away from them with all her might.

To her surprise, Klapon and Klapuf flew across the room and through the wall.

The men groaned as they landed on the grass outside.

Nicole ran for the hole she had made in the wall. She was barely out on the lawn when she heard the third man running after her. "Not so fast, sweetheart. We need you."

A loud clapping sound rang through Nicole's ears before she felt the energy wave that knocked her from her feet. She hit the pavement hard and lost her breath.

Nicole gasped as she tried to get to her feet. What she saw then made her blood run cold.

A robed figure floated down the street toward her. The figure was carrying a circular crystal. "It's the creature from the locker room!" Nicole sobbed. "He's coming to get me."

She tried her best to crawl away, but Klapper caught up to her and dragged the girl to her feet. The combination of abuse and fear made Nicole too weak to struggle. Klapper led her toward the cloaked figure with ease.

The figure lowered its hood, revealing the face of a demon. "I AM SHADOW," it said, holding up the glass ball in its clawed hand. "LOOK INTO THE ORB OF ANACOSTIUM, GIRL." The creature's voice caused Nicole to shake. Klapper's strong hand on her chin forced her to stare at the crystal ball.

A great wind picked up. Nicole barely saw the purple blur that slammed into Klapper, flinging the villain across the lawn and into a stone gnome in the center of a well-manicured garden. He grunted as the gnome shattered over his head.

Without Klapper there to hold her up, Nicole dropped bonelessly to the ground.

Sky Girl landed next to Klapper and examined him. The villain was unconscious. She spotted a garden hose and grabbed it to tie his hands together. She then threw the hose over a tree limb and pulled him off the ground. Sky Girl left the villain suspended from the tree, spinning slowly as he dangled over the lawn. "I like applause as much as the next girl, but that should prevent any unwelcome clapping."

Sky Girl turned to see the cloaked figure moving toward Nicole's prone figure.

With a jump, Sky Girl took to the air, hovering halfway between the victim and the villain. "It's over, Shadow," Sky

Girl said as she put her hands on her hips and slowly descended to the ground.

"IT APPEARS THAT YOU KNOW ME."

Sky Girl tried not cringe at the sound of the creature's voice.

"BUT I ALSO KNOW YOU. YES, I HAVE HEARD OF YOU. SKY GIRL, I PRESUME." The creature moved closer.

"That's right. And you are going down," she said, trying to sound brave, but secretly, Shadow's voice made her want to run away. "Nicole may be a jerk, but she's our jerk and you can't have her."

Sky Girl flew toward Shadow, hoping to end the fight quickly. Instead, she passed right through the creature's cloaks. As she did, she felt intense agony.

The pain was intense; Sky Girl's body spasmed and crashed toward the ground.

Unable to control her descent, Sky Girl smashed into a garbage can.

"APPARENTLY, YOU DO NOT KNOW ENOUGH ABOUT ME, GIRL," Shadow taunted. "YOU CANNOT HARM ME, BUT MY CLOAK OF DARKNESS WILL DESTROY YOU."

From her kneeling position, Sky Girl swung her fist wildly at the creature. Once again, she passed harmlessly through its torso. She screamed in pain. Her eyes rolled up into her head, and she collapsed to the ground.

Shadow turned away from his young attacker and toward his original intended victim.

Nicole was beginning to stir.

Shadow spoke in a mesmerizing tone. "COME, GIRL. LOOK INTO THE ORB AND FULFILL OUR DESTINY."

He made a gesture, and his clawed hand began to glow. "LOOK."

Nicole's eyes glowed as Shadow's spell took control of her mind. She could no longer resist him. The cheerleader turned to stare into the crystal. "Must look," she said in a monotone as she got to her feet.

Sky Girl stirred nearby, forcing herself to wake up. "Have to stop this," she mumbled. "What did those guys in Reading say about Shadow?" She tried to focus on the scene, watching as Nicole looked into the orb.

An idea struck her when she spotted the blinking red light on the telephone pole behind them.

Nicole stared at the glowing green light in the center of the globe. Her eyes began to glow a brighter shade of green.

"Murd, I sure hope you're right," Sky Girl mumbled as she struggled to get her feet, but she couldn't find the strength. The heroine crawled towards the nearby trash bin.

Nicole's could feel her strength as the green light moved from her eyes into the orb.

Sky Girl weakly pulled herself up to her feet on the round metal garbage can.

Nicole had almost surrendered completely to the orb when a silver garbage can lid slammed into it, knocking it to the ground.

"WHAT—?" Shadow exclaimed.

Shadow looked up and saw Sky Girl floating above them, just out of reach of the cloaked demon. "You are a bad man, Shadow. And I think it's time you saw the light!" Sky Girl said weakly as she focused her SkyPulse at the blinking red light on the telephone pole.

The transformer exploded with a loud boom as gold sparks rained down on the street. Every alarm in the neighborhood reacted to the noise. Front and backyard flood lights kicked on in response to the alarm signals, illuminating the expensive estate properties.

New Dover Road and Shadow were bathed in a brilliant white light.

Sky Girl waited for Shadow to react to the light, but nothing happened. "Oh, no!" she lamented. "They were wrong!"

Nicole shook her head as if waking from a dream. She looked at the cloaked figure next to her. "You!" Nicole yelled and kicked him hard in a sensitive area.

Shadow doubled over in pain.

Sky Girl winced.

Nicole raced back into her house and locked the doors.

"They were right. Light is your weakness. It makes you solid." Sky Girl smiled as she flew toward Shadow at SkySpeed. "And if you are solid—" Sky Girl slammed into the cloaked figure and punched him hard. "—I can hit you." She pulled her fist back, ready to strike again. But the creature was already unconscious.

"Lights out, Shadow." Sky Girl looked around and realized she was alone on the street. "Aw, man, I can't believe no one was around to hear that one."

Police sirens blared in the distance. Sky Girl threw Shadow down on the ground and picked up the orb. "Now what am I going to do with you?" Sky Girl asked as her smiled returned.

The police arrived five minutes later and found Shadow tied to a lamppost. Sky Girl had bent the solid steel posts and aimed three spot lights on him. On his chest was a note in very neat handwriting. Little hearts dotted the i's.

Dear Police,

This is a very bad man and badly in need of care and feeding. Please give him bread, water, and especially plenty of light.

TTFN
Sky Girl

P.S.: His buddy is in back. Keep his hands tied together.

#

Ten miles away, DeDe stood in Jason's room at the hospital. She took the orb out of her backpack, where she had placed it after wrapping it carefully in her purple cape.

"This had better work," DeDe said as she squeezed the orb with all of her mighty SkyStrength.

The glass shattered, and green streaks of light shot from the purple cape. One aimed itself at Jason and entered his mouth. He gasped for breath and quickly sat up.

"It is Shadow! Got to tell DeDe!" he shouted as he looked around the room frantically and realized he was in a bed.

DeDe stood next to him, smiling despite the tears streaming down her face.

Jason looked down at his hospital gown and blushed. "What did I miss?"

"I can't believe it," DeDe said as she wiped the tear from her cheek. "I have to face Shadow and Klapper all by myself, and all you did was stay here and take a nap."

"Hey, I was tired," Jason said with a chuckle. He could feel the tears welling up in his eyes, too. "How did you do it? Shadow is the big league."

"Sky Girl got your note and Peter, Murd, and Jamie were able to give her the information needed to help her defeat Shadow."

"Was Bryan there?" Jason asked.

"On vacation with Pant."

Jason laughed. "Just as well. He has a really bad memory and Pants only knows about Flash."

"They wanted me to say 'hi' to Sidekicklad," she whispered.

Jason blushed. "Uh, yeah. That name is...uh...listen, I had better get some rest."

"You're in luck. I'm too tired to give you a hard time."

Jason looked relieved. "Thanks. Goodnight, DeDe."

"Goodnight," she replied as she walked out of the room. A second later she popped her head back through the open doorway and added, with a mischievous grin and an enthusiastic Sky Girl voice, "Sidekicklad!"

Jason turned to throw his pillow at her, but she was gone.

DeDe still wore a grin as she strode down the long, sterile hall of the hospital. She closed her eyes and used her SkyHearing to eavesdrop on the rest of the patients.

All of the cheerleaders had recovered as well. The sounds of joyful celebration echoed down the hallways as Doris and the other rejoiced in the waiting room.

DeDe did not rejoice. She quietly leaned against the wall with her eyes closed, smiled a secret smile, and sighed. "That was a close one."

"What was a close one?" someone asked. DeDe opened her eyes to see Adam staring at her with a goofy grin.

"Um, nothing," DeDe stammered. "Just thinking about how weird this whole night has been."

"This whole town has gotten weird since the gymnasium blew up." Adam observed.

DeDe looked at the ground. "I guess."

"It sounds like everybody is okay," Adam said looking around at the excited hospital staff. "Somebody sure saved the day and deserves our thanks."

DeDe gave Adam a curious look.

"Hey, I wanted to ask you something."

Nicole stormed in, interrupting whatever Adam was about to say. "Help! I need a doctor." She spotted Adam standing with DeDe. "Adam, help me!" Nicole said as she swooned and collapsed into his arms.

He lowered her slowly to the ground, and she looked up at him. "Thank heavens."

Adam shot DeDe a pleading look. "Um, I better . . ."

"Help your girlfriend," DeDe offered uncomfortably.

"But she's ..." Adam looked down at Nicole for a second and then turned back to DeDe.

But, she was gone.

He helped Nicole down the hall and into the emergency room. DeDe watched from around the corner as a small tear streamed down her cheek.

CHAPTER 33

Several Days Later

Jason looked up from his hospital bed and counted the tiles on the ceiling . . . again. It was his fifth time doing so in an hour, and there were still thirty tiles.

Jason sat up in the bed and checked the small clock on the dresser. It was a little after seven at night. He thought about DeDe and pouted.

Sky Girl had solved the mystery of Shadow on her own, leaving Jason feeling less than worthless. He realized he was wallowing again and turned over in the bed. He still felt useless. DeDe would surely mock him for it if she knew.

He rolled to his back and decided to count the ceiling tiles again.

As if on cue, Jason heard a beeping noise coming from his bedside dresser. Jason leaned off the side of the bed and used his leg to push the hospital room door closed. "That is better," he said proudly as he opened the dresser drawer and took out the small earpiece DeDe had brought him. He was glad the device was working again.

"What is up, DeDe?" Jason whispered.

"Hey," DeDe's voice said through his ear piece. He mentally corrected himself. Her voice was lower; she was Sky Girl. There was also a lot of background noise and static. "You're not going to believe this."

"I am lying in a hospital bed because a demon called Shadow sucked my soul into the Orb of Anacostium. I would like to think I have learned to be fairly open-minded. Try me."

Sky Girl chuckled over the earpiece. "I'm serious. I saw another flying girl."

"Really? Where?"

"I was over by the Woodbridge Center Mall this afternoon, and I saw her fly over the parking lot. Oh, and I also saw these really cool purple workout pants." Her voice raised an octave and sounded much more like DeDe's.

"Sky Girl voice," Jason interrupted in a stern voice.

"Oops, sorry," Sky Girl answered in a deeper voice.

"Where is she now?" Jason asked as he reached for his backpack near the bed.

He opened the front pouch and rifled through several comic books and magazines. Finally, he pulled out his SkyBoy handbook, gently removing the book from its Mylar bag.

"About five hundred feet below me," Sky Girl answered. "I followed her from the mall."

"Most excellent." He took out a pen. "What is she wearing?"

"Uh oh. She saw me and is landing."

"Wait! Do not follow her. We need to find who she is first. We have to play this right. Be subtle. Do not draw attention to yourself. Stay hidden."

"Hi. I'm Sky Girl," Jason heard his friend say through the radio with a cheerful tone. "So, um, who are you?"

He dropped his head to his hands and sighed; so much for subtlety. "Or you could just ignore everything I said and introduce yourself." Jason continued to listen to the girls' conversation through the earpiece.

"I'm Penny Pound," the other girl said in a thick English accident.

Jason flipped through the book until he reached P. There was no Penny Pound.

"Sky Girl, I cannot find any Penny Pound, but there is a British villain who was called Pence Pound," he said, alarmed. "He had strength, invulnerability, and flight."

"So are you a bad guy or what?" Penny Pound asked, her voice becoming tense.

"Funny," Sky Girl responded, "I was going to ask you the same thing."

"I think you should stop her as fast as you can. We can figure out who she is after," Jason said as he skimmed the entry, looking for some sort of weakness.

"That's a really nice handbag," Sky Girl said.

Jason was confused as he listened to the conversation on the earpiece. "This is not how this is supposed to work."

"I got it in Paris at this little shop on the Champs Élysées. I really like your boots. They match your mask perfectly."

"Thanks. I got them in the mall we were at. I could show you where I bought them. They were white originally. Dying them purple was a real pain."

"I know," Penny Pound responded in a cheerful voice. "Do you have any idea how many times I had to dye this belt to get the right shade of red?"

Jason was absolutely appalled. His heroes never acted like this in the comic books. "Uh, Sky Girl? Are you going to fight or what?"

"Huh?" Sky Girl responded, confused. "Oh, I forgot. I'll ask. So are we gonna fight? Just to let you know, I'm not the bad guy here."

There was a long silence. Jason tried to stay calm. "DeDe, I am not sure that you are playing this right."

"Well, that's great!" Penny chimed. "I'm not the bad guy either."

"Excellent," Sky Girl said. "So what's your story?"

"That's a fair question. I could use your help." Penny Pound laughed but then added, "But first, DeDe, we should pick up your friend that has been talking in your ear. I believe you called him Jason when you were following me."

"What?" Jason gasped. He looked down at the listing for Pence Pound and realized he had missed that enhanced hearing was listed.

Penny Pound laughed. "Oh, relax. You Americans, with your secrets. Don't worry. I won't tell a soul."

"Oh, yeah? Then what's your real name?" Sky Girl asked.

"I told you, silly. My name is Penny Pound."

Jason sighed. "Bring her over to the hospital," he said, resigned to the fact that Penny Pound knew their secret. "I will meet you in the courtyard out back."

"That works for me," Penny Pound said, overhearing everything. "And please tell Jason that Pence Pound was my father."

"I cannot believe they did not fight first." Jason shook his head in disbelief as he reached for his pants. "No respect for tradition."

CHAPTER 34

A half hour later, Jason sat on a bench in the hospital courtyard and updated his notes on Pence and Penny Pound.

The courtyard was completely covered by trees, allowing for optimal privacy. When he'd first arrived, he'd scouted the area to ensure there was no one around and, more importantly, to ensure there were no hidden security cameras.

The area was secure.

Jason heard the sound of rushing air and looked up from his notebook.

A second later, Sky Girl and Penny Pound landed in the clearing. Sky Girl was dressed in her usual costume.

Jason was more taken by the blonde girl standing next to Sky Girl. At six feet, Penny Pound stood a foot taller than Sky Girl. Her shoulder-length blonde hair blew in the night air and accented her muscular shoulders. She wore what appeared to be a white one-piece swimsuit with the Union Jack flag of Great Britain silk-screened across her large chest, at which Jason immediately realized he was staring. He quickly looked up and into Penny Pound's crystal blue eyes, which were visible behind her red leather mask. Around her waist was a red leather sash, which she had tied on her left side. It blew in the wind in a cool eighties comics kind of way.

"Wow, great costume," he said, somewhat awe-struck by her.

"Sky Girl, you didn't mention how cute your friend is," Penny Pound said in her English accent as she brushed her red-gloved hand across Jason's cheek.

"Whatevs," Sky Girl said, somewhat annoyed. "So what's your story?"

Jason took out his notebook, and Penny Pound eyed him suspiciously. "Do not mind me. I usually do not have an opportunity to take notes. You are the first super-powered person I have met besides DeDe that has not tried to kill me."

"Well, not yet, anyway, but it's still early," Sky Girl mumbled under her breath.

"So cute," Penny Pound repeated, tousling Jason's blonde hair with her red glove. "Well my story's not too complicated. My dad was Pence Pound. After I was born, he decided to give up crime and reformed." Her voice softened. "When I got older, we found I had inherited his powers. We teamed up and fought crime as father and daughter in London."

"Where's your father now?" Sky Girl tried not to sound jealous of Penny Pound's relationship with her father.

Penny's eyes began to tear up, and she sunk down to sit on the bench. "He was murdered." Her voice cracked as she choked out the words.

Sky Girl put her purple-gloved hand on Penny Pound's shoulder and sat down next to her. "I'm sorry. I lost my dad, too."

There was silence for a moment as the girls shared a moment. Penny wiped her wet eyes and stood up. "That's why I need your help. I followed Father's killer from London, across the pound to Colonia. I think he's still here. I was looking for him when I saw your beautiful shopping arcade."

"And that is where you met Sky Girl," Jason said as he made another notation.

"Yes, and now that I have, you can assist me and we'll find my father's killer," Penny Pound said with determination, "And deal with the Wag once and for all."

"The Wag?" Jason asked, shocked. He still was not used to the fact that these villains were real. "Whoa."

"Who or what is a Wag?" Sky Girl asked concerned by Jason's reaction. "Sounds like some kind of dog? Is this another dog?"

"Not *a* Wag—*the* Wag," he corrected. "He was one of SkyBoy's heavy-hitter villains."

DeDe noted that this was the first villain Jason did not need to look up in the *OHUS*.

"No one really knows his origin. He is absolutely insane and has the power to make people around him crazy, too." Jason paused added solemnly, "He is a mass murderer."

Sky Girl's mouth hung open. "But I thought nobody died in your comics."

Jason slowly shook his head. "The Wag is the obvious exception to that rule. He is a crazy serial killer."

"Don't worry." Sky Girl turned to Penny Pound. "If he's here, we'll find him. And we'll stop him together."

Penny Pound's eyes welled up with tears again. "Thank you."

The two heroines hugged as Jason looked on and cleared his throat. "Um, as fascinating and enjoyable as this is, it is getting late." His voice cracked, which made both girls giggle. He ignored them. "How can we find you if we need to talk?"

Penny gave Jason a small card and spoke in a whisper. "Go to this address. There's a large searchlight on the roof that flashes a pound sign into the sky. Use the Pound Signal and I will come."

Jason studied the card. "Really?"

Penny laughed. "Of course not, silly. That's my hotel address. I am staying at the Galietti." She slowly started to float off the ground, making eye contact with Jason. "Call me if you want to talk. Or something."

Jason blushed brightly as he nodded in the affirmative.

"Um, under what name are you staying?" Sky Girl asked.

She chuckled again. "Silly secretive Americans. I'm staying under my name: Penny Pound." A second later, she flew off into the night sky, leaving a red streak behind her.

"What do you think, Sky Girl?" Jason turned to his friend, but she had already changed. DeDe was standing next to him.

"Well, she was telling the truth," DeDe said, as she shoved the cape into her duffle bag. "I used my SkyVision on her the whole time she was talking. She never turned pink."

Jason smiled with pride. With practice, DeDe had learned to use her special SkyVision, which had a useful side effect. It also worked as a lie detector. "I was going to suggest that, but I was afraid Penny would overhear me. So, um, she was telling the truth the whole time?"

DeDe was initially confused, but then she understood his real question and rolled her eyes. "Sheesh. Yes, Jason, Penny

Pound was telling the truth when she said she thought you were cute."

"Cool," he said before returning to business. "Well, I get out of here tomorrow. When I get home, I will do some research on the Wag to see if there are any weaknesses I do not know about."

"But now—" DeDe yawned. "—I have to get home. I have an all-day AP chemistry midterm, and I still have to do the calculus homework." In the blink of an eye, DeDe Christopher was gone and Sky Girl stood in her place in front of Jason.

"Unless you want to do the homework for me."

Jason gave her a condescending look.

"Hey, it was worth a try," Sky Girl said before she took the hint and flew off into the night sky.

"She thought I was cute," Jason said with a smile before he exited the courtyard to return to his hospital room.

#

Across town, Penny Pound had already arrived at the Galietti Hotel. The heroine landed on the balcony and opened the sliding glass door to her luxurious hotel suite.

A large green and red bird jumped around its cage and welcomed the young heroine home.

"Goodness, that boy was cute, Ms. Amy," Penny Pound said to the brightly plumed bird as she adjusted the bird feeder. She kicked off her boots and gloves and tossed them on the bed, then took off her mask and threw it on the table.

"Cute boy," the parrot responded.

"Yes, very cute." Penny smiled back.

At that moment, someone knocked on the door. Penny picked up an expensive robe off the couch and put it on over her cape and white unitard. After making sure her costume was completely covered, Penny walked over and answered the door.

A man in a white coat did not wait to be invited in before he entered the room. He pushed a service cart ahead of him. "Room Service!"

"I didn't order room service."

"It is part of a new contest." The man had a large black handlebar mustache, which made him look quite comical. "If you answer the following question correctly, then your meal is free." He made an exaggerated gesture to the cart. "Get it wrong, and you will have to pay."

Penny Pound smiled at the man's theatrics. "Okay, I'll give it a try."

He took out a small card and read it aloud. "Think of words ending in -gry. Angry and hungry are two of them. There are only three words in the English language. What is the third word? The word is something that everyone uses every day. If you have listened carefully, I have already told you what it is."

"I have no idea," Penny said with a giggle.

The man looked up from his cue card. "Oh, I am sorry. We were looking for *language*. Language is definitely something most people use every day, and in the phrase 'the English language,' it is the third word. You lose and now must pay!"

A loud crash sounded as the cart blew up in Penny's face.

The force of the explosion knocked her to the ground and shredded her robe, revealing her costume underneath. Penny struggled to lift her head and look up at the man. The room started to spin as she blacked out.

"Some . . . kind of . . . gas," she said as she closed her eyes and laid her head down on the carpeted floor. "Are you the Wag?" she asked with her remaining strength.

"Wrong again," the funny man exclaimed. "But the Wag is my employer. I am the QuizMaster. And you, Penny Pound, are now my prisoner."

Penny barely heard the man gloat because she was almost unconscious. Her vision dimmed as she watched the villain drop something on the table. He gathered her gloves, boots, and mask and placed them in a bag.

Penny was sure she could hear Amy squawking, "QuizMaster! QuizMaster!"

Then Penny heard nothing at all as she completely blacked out, her head dropping down on the luxurious carpet.

CHAPTER 35

Jason's mother sat in the driver's side of their family Prius and cried.

"Ma, I am fine," Jason repeated. "The doctors gave me a clean bill of health." He adjusted his black *Slaughtered Lamb* sweatshirt and tried to look healthy.

"Nonsense!" Doris replied as she pulled a tissue out of her Hawaiian print muumuu. "I just checked my baby out of the hospital. I am not dropping you off at the mall."

"Ma!" Jason whined. "It is book day." He did his best to muster one of the puppy dog looks DeDe had perfected. When he saw how ridiculous he looked in the rearview mirror, he stopped. "You do not want me to miss book day!"

"Fine. I'll drop you off at the mall. But you need to call me if you feel even a little bit sick."

"I promise." Jason held his hand up in an Eagle Scout salute. "I should be home for dinner."

Tears welled up in Doris' eyes again. "My baby is getting so big."

Jason put his hands through his hair. "Ma!"

Doris pulled the car into the mall parking lot. Although Jason saw his mother lick her hand as she pulled into the drop-off zone, he wasn't fast enough.

She used her hand to smooth down her son's unkempt hair before he got out of the car. Jason shrieked as he exited the vehicle. "Ma!"

He waved as his mother drove off, watching as the car rounded the corner. A second later, he hailed a taxi and instructed the driver to take him over to the Galietti Hotel.

On the ride over, he called DeDe's cell phone, but it jumped straight to voicemail. "Hey, DeDe. I thought I would get you before the test. Do not worry; it is nothing important. I am heading over to try to meet with our old friend. I have some follow-up questions for her." Jason did not mention the fact that she was attractive and thought he was cute was an added incentive for the meeting. "I will call you when I know more."

As the cab approached the Galietti Hotel, Jason saw the flashing lights of police cars parked in front of the hotel. He paid the driver and quickly exited the taxi, then rushed into the lobby. Two policemen were talking at the front desk, and Jason edged a little closer so he could overhear their conversation.

"Any idea where she is?" the first officer asked.

"I don't know. Some British rocker or something, I guess. She trashed room 213 on the second floor and left. There ain't no sign of Ms. Pound."

"Penny!" Jason whispered in alarm. He raced across the lobby and into the stairwell, sprinting up the stairs to the second floor. His pulse pounded as he tried to catch his breath.

He slowly opened the fire door and peered out onto the second floor, exhaling in relief when the hallway was empty.

Police tape blocked access to the room at the end of the long hallway. He walked down to the doorway of room 213 and peered in past the tape. The room was vacant except for a parrot in a golden cage.

"Hello?" he called out.

No one responded.

Jason lifted the yellow caution tape and entered the room. "There must be something they missed—some kind of clue as to what happened."

Jason examined the room. There were an overturned table and a half-finished crossword puzzle on the ground but not much else. He dialed DeDe's phone and got her voicemail again. "Our friend is in trouble," he said. "I am here in her hotel room. I do not understand it. There is nothing consistent with what I know about the Wag." Jason hung up the phone and looked at the bird. "I do not suppose you saw what happened to Penny," he said absentmindedly. "Who could have done this?"

"QuizMaster," the bird squawked again.

"What?" Jason said, turning to the bird.

"QuizMaster has you now. Ha ha ha!" the bird chirped.

"QuizMaster?" Jason immediately knew the name. He tried to remember what he knew about the villain.

He paced the room and talked to himself as the bird chirped away, happily eating its seed. "Let me see. Blink Bark was an out-of-work game show host. An insane genius, he had a warped sense of honor and would only attack people who could not answer his questions. He did not do it because he wanted to. It was a psychological compulsion—he needed to leave clues."

"He needed to leave clues." Jason pounded his forehead. "I have been looking at this all wrong."

He examined the room again. This time when he saw the crossword puzzle, he walked over and picked it up. Someone had filled out the top half of the puzzle.

He looked at the filled-in blocks. He hoped the words would provide a clue. Unfortunately, someone had just written random letters in the boxes. He ruled that out, then tried to read the clues but found that they were also written in gibberish.

Jason sat in a chair in the corner of the room. He looked at the puzzle again, certain it was a clue, but the questions meant nothing. The answers meant nothing.

He walked to the closet, took out a phone book, and turned to a map in the back. Then he saw the solution. The clue was not in the puzzle; it was the puzzle itself. He took out his cell phone and dialed DeDe. Once again, her voicemail picked up. Jason looked at his watch before leaving his message.

"Hey, DeDe. It is Jason. I assume you are in your chemistry test for the next couple of hours. Something happened. I lost my contact. I think someone took it and I am going to look for it at. . . " He paused and realized this was not the time to be cute. "Tell Sky Girl that QuizMaster kidnapped Penny Pound. I am going to the old television studio on the corner where Half-Full Avenue crosses Word Street. I think that is where he is holding her. Have Sky Girl come as soon as she can."

Jason hung up. "I hope I am not too late to save Penny Pound."

After he had run from the room, the bird happily chirped, "Cute boy."

CHAPTER 36

Jason looked up a faded sign that showed the defunct call letters of WWIG. WWIG Channel 68 had been one of the preeminent privately owned television stations; however, since the advent of cable and satellite television, the local access UHF station had fallen out of favor. Jason remembered watching the channel for old episodes of *Soupy Sales*, *Speed Racer*, *Hercules*, and *Battle of the Planets* on the staticky black-and-white television set in his kitchen. Unable to compete with large network programming, WWIG had closed its doors ten years ago.

He approached the door of the long-abandoned television station and turned the knob. It was unlocked. He pushed on the door and it slowly creaked open.

Jason peered inside and got his second surprise. He had expected a dusty, rundown facility. Instead, the set was active and brightly lit with a myriad of flashing lights. The theme song from an old game show played faintly in the background.

He called DeDe again. Once again, her cell phone jumped directly to voicemail. Jason took a deep breath and entered the studio. He walked toward the music and entered an old soundstage with seating for a studio audience, sneaking in as quietly as possible.

He ducked down and hid in the last row of audience seating.

A bright red carpet covered four steps that led to the stage. Jason gasped when he saw what was there.

Penny Pound, dressed in her costume and mask, was encased in a glowing bubble that looked very cramped. Jason surmised that her powers were somehow negated since the bubble appeared to be made of simple glass. QuizMaster stood at a podium, dressed in a bright yellow sequined tuxedo.

"I'm sorry, Penny Pound, but once again, that is the wrong answer." Quizmaster pressed a button on the podium, and the glass globe cage shrank. Penny winced in pain and contorted her body to try to fit into the smaller space.

"I dare say that if you get one more wrong, I believe this game will be over. Far too quickly for my tastes, I might add." QuizMaster spoke with a genuine sadness. He took out another card. "Tintinnabulation means the ringing of a bell, but it also has a unique spelling. Please spell it."

Penny spoke in a weak whisper. "T–I—"

With no time to waste, Jason jumped out from his hiding space and stepped into the aisle. "It is spelled I-T. I believe that is the answer you are looking for, Quizmaster."

A spotlight shone on Jason, and the step beneath him lit up white.

"Hey! No help from the studio audience. Who are you, anyway? A would-be savior?" QuizMaster asked with a sneer. "I do not believe you were invited to be on my show."

"I am Jason, and I was not invited." His eyes met Penny's. He could almost feel her pain as he gazed into her crystal blue eyes. "And yes, I am here to rescue Penny Pound." He looked back at QuizMaster. "Unless you are afraid to face me in a trivia battle of wits."

QuizMaster pondered for a moment but took the challenge. He spoke in an announcer's voice. "Very well. Welcome to the show, Jason. Here's how the game is played. I will ask a series of questions. For each correct answer, you advance one step. If you get it wrong, Pretty Penny Pound's prison pinches and shrinks. In the unlikely event you make it to the stage, you get to ask me a question. If I can't answer, I will let you and Penny Pound go free. If I answer it, you join her in the bubble prison and the game begins anew." The sounds of canned applause filled the studio.

Jason nodded in assent.

Quizmaster laughed. "Excellent! Now let's see if you were correct."

Jason held his breath and hoped he had answered the question correctly. When the step he was standing on turned green, he breathed a sigh of relief. Jason advanced to the next step.

Quizmaster took out a card. "Very good. Now for your next question, Jason."

"Excuse me?" he asked politely. "I answered two other questions; I should move forward two more spaces."

"What?" QuizMaster said in surprise. "I do not think so."

"Respectfully, sir," Jason said with as much politeness as he could muster, "first, you asked me to spell 'it,' then you asked who I was, and then you asked if I was some sort of savior. I believe I answered all three."

QuizMaster stood dumbstruck, apparently trying to find a way around the logical loophole he had created. Finally,

Quizmaster spoke. "The judges have considered your request and you—" The villain paused for dramatic effect. "—are correct. Please advance two spaces."

The steps in front of Jason turned green, leaving him just two questions away from Penny. He looked at his watch. There was still almost an hour left before DeDe's test was over. He needed to stall.

"I have a question," he said.

"I am sorry. You must reach the stage first," Quizmaster responded as he looked at the card and read the next question. "The Great Forest is a scary place. It is one hundred meters long. There is a town called Lau that borders the forest. The Lauians are a brave people. How far can the bravest Lauian venture into the great forest?"

Jason thought for a moment, then smiled. "Fifty meters. Because once they are halfway in, they are venturing out of the great forest."

QuizMaster was clearly impressed. "That is correct."

The last step lit up, and Jason stepped onto the stage.

"You have made it farther than any other contestant." QuizMaster took out the final card. "When the day after tomorrow is yesterday, today will be as far from Wednesday as today was from Wednesday when the day before yesterday was tomorrow. What is the day after this day? "

It was relatively straightforward, but it took Jason a moment to puzzle it out. Finally, he said, "Thursday. The answer is Thursday."

"Is that your final answer?"

Jason nodded, and the applause track went wild.

"That is correct," said QuizMaster

Balloons and confetti fell to the stage. Penny Pound gave a weak smile.

"Now, young, heroic Jason," QuizMaster said. "You may ask your one question."

Jason thought for a moment. "Okay, you are on a bus, and there are three passengers on it plus you."

"Excellent. A bus mathematics question," QuizMaster said with glee. "These are my favorites."

"At the first stop, three passengers get on and two get off. And the next stop, five get on and one gets off. At the last stop, all but the driver get off," Jason said as he looked at QuizMaster, his voice starting to quiver with nervousness. "What is the name of the person left on the bus?"

"What? How should I know?" QuizMaster frowned. "No, wait. There must be an answer. Statistically, John is the most common name. So it must be John. No, wait. Bus drivers are blue collar workers. So he would not be John. He would be Jack. The bus driver's name is Jack." He smiled at his own cleverness.

"Wrong!" Jason exclaimed "The bus driver's name is Blink Bark, the QuizMaster. I said there were three passengers and you, therefore—"

"I was driving the bus, You beat me!" QuizMaster picked up a futuristic-looking control and aimed it at Jason. "And I hate to lose." He pressed the button, and Jason winced.

Nothing happened to him.

Instead, Penny's cage disappeared; the heroine tumbled to the floor, and Jason ran to her side.

"I am bound by my rules. A deal is a deal. You are free to go," QuizMaster said, pointing at the door. "For today."

"Let's go," Penny said weakly as Jason helped her up off the floor of the stage. "He works for the Wag."

"Not yet. If we go now, he will never leave us alone. QuizMaster, I challenge you. I will let you try to answer one more question. Double or nothing. You get it right, and we both get in the bubble. You get it wrong, you turn yourself in."

QuizMaster's eyes lit up at the second chance. As Jason suspected, he really hated to lose. "Agreed!"

Jason tried to remember what he could about SkyBoy's rogue gallery. He knew that QuizMaster captured Penny Pound at the behest of the Wag. Suddenly, he had a plan. He hoped he was correct.

"What is the secret identity of the Wag?"

QuizMaster looked upset. "What? The Wag? You fool. That one is easy. You have doomed yourself and Penny Pound. I know that the real name of the Wag is Ju—Jud—"

QuizMaster never finished the answer. Instead, he began to laugh hysterically. Within seconds, the villain was doubled over in maniacal laughter. He fell to the stage and continued to laugh uncontrollably.

Finally, QuizMaster stopped moving all together. Jason was relieved to see that the villain was at least still breathing.

Penny Pound leaned on Jason as they stared in silence at the still man on the stage.

"I think we won," Jason said with a smile.

"Is he dead? Did you kill him?"

"Oh, no. I think he has just laughed himself unconscious. Still, we should get out of here. You know, just in case."

A large crashing noise interrupted them as Sky Girl smashed through the ceiling. "Okay, QuizMaster, the game is up," she said menacingly. Sky Girl landed on the stage and looked at the unconscious villain, then at Jason and Penny. "Or it was up before I got here?"

"It is okay. We got this one," Jason said with a smile. "Still, cool entrance! I like the way you played on the QuizMaster angle with your whole 'the game is up' line."

Sky Girl grinned. "Yeah, I worked on the banter on the way over. Now, does one of you want to tell me what happened?" Sirens sounded in the distance. "After we get out of here, I guess.

#

When the police arrived a few minutes later, they found QuizMaster tied up on the stage with a note pinned to his chest. DeDe's trademark hearts dotted the I's.

Hey Police Dudes,
This guy kidnapped Penny Pound and really likes to play games. Please sign him up for the prison chess club.

TTFN
Sky Girl.

#

Later that afternoon, DeDe, Penny, and Jason sat in a booth at the Colonia diner across town. Jason had just finished his story and his second order of cheese fries. DeDe tried not to notice that Penny was holding Jason's hand under the table.

"I don't get it. How did you know what would happen to Quizmaster?"

"I wondered that myself, cutie," Penny added as she stroked Jason's cheek.

"Well, I remembered in an old issue of SkyBoy—I think it was part one of the—"

"Snore!" DeDe said loudly.

Penny giggled.

"Fine," Jason said, annoyed. "It was a story with the Wag in it. The Wag bragged that he always used his power to prevent any of his henchmen from divulging his secrets. There was a lot of monologuing in comics back then. I asked him who the Wag really was. When he tried to answer, he began to laugh uncontrollably because he was under the Wag's power."

"My hero!" Penny exclaimed as she hugged Jason.

"Yeah, my hero," DeDe repeated as she rolled her eyes.

Penny stood up. "But I never found the Wag. I guess he wasn't here after all. It was all a trap."

"What will you do now?" Jason asked, standing up next to her.

"I couldn't find any clues about the Wag here. I guess I'll head back to England and continue my search." She handed Jason a piece of paper with her phone number on it.

"We'll keep an eye out for the Wag. We have your number if something turns up," DeDe said.

Penny leaned in to DeDe and kissed her on the cheek. "Thank you, Sky Girl."

"Hey, what about me?" Jason whined.

"And you," Penny said as she leaned in and gave Jason a long kiss on the lips. She bit his lip before pulling away. "I expect you to call me every chance you get, cutie pie. You're not getting away from me that easily."

Jason was giddy as Penny left the diner. He stumbled back into the booth, still smiling.

DeDe gave him a cross look.

"What? What did I do?"

Before DeDe could answer, Adam walked into the diner with the rest of the football team. While the rest of the team sat down, Adam stopped in front of Jason and DeDe's booth. "Hey, DeDe. Can I talk to you for a minute?"

Jason stood up. "I am going to, uh, look at the jukebox. I wonder if they have updated the music since 1984."

Adam sat down in the booth and stretched out his muscular biceps. "Hey, DeDe."

DeDe smiled. "Hey, Adam. You said that already. Where's Nicole?"

Adam appeared uncomfortable at the mention of Nicole. "Um, she's in Europe with her dad. He had business or something. He goes there a lot."

There was a long silence before Adam spoke again. "Listen, I know you and Nicole are, like, really close."

DeDe tried not to laugh out loud.

"But I wanted to let you know that it's over between her and me. It kind of has been for a while."

"Really?" DeDe asked in surprise. "What happened?"

Adam fidgeted in his seat. "Yeah. Since last year at the nationals. When I realized..." He trailed off again.

DeDe tried not to be too happy about the breakup. "That's too bad. You and Nicole were—"

Adam interrupted before his courage waned. "You and I have gotten kind of close lately, and I didn't want to let this thing with Nicole hurt our friendship. You are important to me, and I really like you, DeDe."

Shocked into silence, she could only nod in agreement.

He edged his way out of the booth. "Listen, I'd better go sit with the team. I have your number and will give you a call. Maybe we can hang sometime. You know, like a movie or . . ."

"You mean like a date or something."

Adam blushed and looked down. "Yeah, like a date. What do you say?"

"I say yes. I would love to."

"Great!" he exclaimed. "I'll call you."

DeDe watched him stumble out of the booth and join his friends. Several of them gave Adam high fives. He looked back at DeDe, clearly embarrassed by the attention.

Jason returned from the juke box to move back into his seat in the booth. "Yep. They still have the same songs. I swear, it is like all music stopped after Footloose," he joked.

DeDe did not hear him as she stared off into space with a goofy grin on her face.

After a moment, she noticed Jason giving her the same look she had shot him moments before, right after Penny Pound had kissed him.

"What?" she asked with a smile.

"Nothing," Jason said as he signaled for the check. "I think things are looking up for both of us."

CHAPTER 37

The Next Week

"This is so not fair," DeDe said as she floated upside down in the basement of 16 Hartland Court. Her purple sweatshirt hung down over her pouting face, revealing the silver dance leotard underneath. As the teen bobbed up and down, her red hair scraped the floor of the basement.

"It was bound to happen," Jason said matter-of-factly. He was sitting on the couch and wore ripped jeans and a t-shirt that said *Real men don't set for stun*. He didn't even bother to look up from reading the latest issue of *The Journey of Jersey Devil* to address his best friend.

He had been through this kind of drama with her before. He knew that DeDe's latest temper tantrum would pass, and then they could hopefully have an intelligent conversation on the subject afterwards.

"I guess. But still," DeDe added under her breath, "it's just not fair."

She focused her eyes and put her hand out. Her nose crunched up as she strained her face. A small, multi-colored net appeared in the air in front of her, flickering for a moment before it fizzled. "I can't even do the SkyNet thingie."

"Electronet," Jason corrected. "Relax. The Electronet is tied to your focused emotions. You are hardly the poster child for focus right now."

DeDe screamed in frustration. "First the whole thing with Gronk and the Protectorate, and now this!" DeDe floated up to the top of the room, put her feet on the ceiling, and crossed her arms indignantly.

Jason put down the book and stood eye-to-eye with the upside-down DeDe. "I still do not think I really get it. Can you tell me the story again?"

DeDe sighed heavily as she thought back on her evening, preparing to tell Jason the story again as she paced across the ceiling. Jason looked on as if it were perfectly normal.

#

Sky Girl had just landed behind some large bushes in front of her house, returning from another unsuccessful patrol. She and Jason had continued to perform systematic searches of the area in an attempt to locate Gronk. She had just finished searching the nearby Roosevelt Park for the creature on the assumption that the area would be less populated.

Although Sky Girl was able to stop a mugging, pull someone from a burning car, and even help a cat out of a tree, there was no sign of Gronk. After two hours, she gave up looking and flew home.

Frustrated by the whole situation, she could certainly have used the Protectorate's help but knew she could not ask for it.

She was still angry at them, plus she had no idea what they would do to Gronk if the Protectorate found him.

The entire situation was confusing.

And then there was the whole Adam thing.

She crouched down in the bushes and moved at SkySpeed to change out of her costume and into a silver leotard and purple sweatsuit. A moment later, DeDe moved out of the bushes with her purple backpack and climbed the steps of 16 Hartland Court. She stood in front of the blue door and fumbled for her keys. As she did, she thought of Adam.

In the week since he'd told her about breaking up with Nicole, he had paid more attention to her—a lot more. He'd called pretty much every night. They were even going on a real date in a few days. DeDe sighed and reached down to put her key in the lock, but she hadn't realized she was floating above the ground.

"Oops," she said, forcing herself back down to the ground. Jason had to remind her now more than ever to stop floating and stay on the ground.

When she landed, she flung open the front door and ran upstairs. As she did, DeDe tossed her purple backpack into her room. She held her hands up in triumph. "Score!"

"Mom, I'm home!" she called down the hall as she entered the house, but no one was there.

A note sat on the kitchen table next to the cookie jar. DeDe grabbed a large chocolate chip cookie and shoved it into her mouth before picking up the note.

She read it out loud with the cookie in her mouth.

Daughter DeDe,

I have gone shopping with Mrs. Shewstal and then am meeting Michael for dinner at La Sherrier. Roll-ups are in the oven. Don't wait up.

Love, Mother Dianne

PS: Get that cookie out of your mouth. You will spoil your dinner."

DeDe gulped as she swallowed the cookie, wondering if perhaps she wasn't the only one in the house with superpowers.

DeDe opened the oven to fetch her dinner. While she ate roll-ups, her mother would be enjoying La Sherrier, one of the fanciest restaurants in town. No wonder she had gone dress shopping. DeDe reached into the open oven and grabbed the glass plate with her bare hand. "Smells delicious," she said to the empty house as she put the plate on the table. A sizzling sound reminded her of the heat as the broiling hot dish began to melt the Corian countertop.

"Oops." She quickly grabbed the scalding plate and put a trivet under it. DeDe smiled. She hadn't had to use a potholder since before the Nationals.

Just then DeDe heard a noise coming from downstairs. Using her SkyHearing, DeDe focused on the noise.

Someone breathing downstairs.

Someone was in the house.

Jason had warned her that the Protectorate might come after her after what had happened with Gronk—not to mention the increasing number of villains she had encountered, or how poor Penny Pound had been attacked in her hotel room. She searched for her backpack before realizing she had thrown it into her bedroom. "I hope I'm fast enough," she mumbled.

DeDe rushed down the stairs at SkySpeed and tackled the intruder, easily throwing him to the floor with a loud *whump*.

A male voice groaned. "DeDe?"

She immediately recognized his voice before the speaker could identify himself.

"It's Michael." Her mother's boyfriend was dressed in elegant formalwear. He lay there for a moment, his black tuxedo covered in dust. The situation would have been hilarious under other circumstances.

This was not one of them.

"Oh my gosh! Mr. Valjorge, I'm so sorry," she said, helping him up.

"Good golly, you dancers are tough," he joked as he took her hand. "I'm just getting my second wind."

DeDe turned crimson. "Sorry. I was scared. Mom's not home and—"

"DeDe," Michael interrupted, "It's okay." He looked at the floor as though searching for something. "I just wanted to talk to you about something."

DeDe used her SkyVision to find the little blue box on the ground and scooped it up. "Is this what you're looking for?" She said as she examined the box.

The cube was about two inches wide, high, and deep. The letters T-I-F-F could be seen embossed on the top of the box underneath an elegantly tied white ribbon. DeDe did not need to use her SkyVision to know what was inside.

She gasped as she handed him the box.

"Thanks. That's kind of what I wanted to talk to you about."

"It's a ring. Are you . . . and mom getting married?" she stammered.

"Only if she says yes," Michael said with a nervous chuckle. His faced flushed. He quickly added, "And with your blessing."

DeDe paused for a moment. Finally, she said, "Um,, sure. Why not?"

Michael shook her hand. "I'd better get going; I have a lot of things to plan," he called as he rushed out of the basement.

DeDe stood in the dark and watched him leave.

#

That had been two hours ago. An emergency call had brought Jason over with a run.

Since then she had been in the basement, pouting. "'Sure.' I can't believe I just said, 'Sure. Why not?' when I should have screamed 'No!'"

Jason smiled at the melodrama that was his best friend. "It is going to be okay," he said for the tenth time. He didn't even bother looking up from his *Journey of the Jersey Devil* comic.

"No, it's not. My life is over." DeDe slowly floated through a back flip and landed on the floor. "C'mon!" She grabbed her overcoat from a hook in the corner.

Jason picked up his coat slowly. He had learned long ago that he did not like it when DeDe used that tone of voice. "Where are we going?"

"To see someone who will understand."

"But it is dark out, and it could be dangerous." Jason knew where they were going and did not like it. "And I did not finish my comic. It is a new, edgier take on Jersey Devil written by Neil Gaim—"

DeDe interrupted him with an "Are you serious?" look and stormed out the basement door. "What could happen?"

"Fine! But I am bringing the suit. Just in case." Reluctantly, Jason picked up DeDe's purple backpack and followed her out the door and into the yard. "Your 'what-could-happen' situations have a bad habit of turning into, 'You will not believe what happened.'"

CHAPTER 38

Colonia Memorial Gardens was located on the opposite side of town from DeDe's house. There were very few lampposts in the cemetery, providing very little illumination on the graveyard. Instead, the white marble of the tombstones and mausoleums reflected the light of the full moon. The effect served to create an eerie glow on the gravel walkways, which enhanced the creepiness of the place.

Established in 1910, the cemetery contained heroes from four wars. DeDe couldn't care less about those people.

What mattered to DeDe was that the cemetery also contained the grave of Cain Christopher, her father.

She couldn't remember when she'd first visited the cemetery. She was too little to remember the day they buried her father. It wasn't until several years later that she and Jason had discovered the wooded trails that led into the back side of the graveyard. DeDe had ridden her Big Wheel into the cemetery with Jason following on his Green Machine. They'd searched for hours, driving across the manicured lawn until she found the marble tombstone that marked her daddy's grave.

She remembered how it towered above her and Jason. She'd simply stood there and stared at the grave in silence, holding Jason's hand, until the sun went down. Finally, Jason had become too frightened, and DeDe had agreed to take him home.

In many ways, that had been Jason's and her first adventure together.

Since then, DeDe had dragged her best friend to Colonia Memorial Gardens many times, first on tricycles, then on bicycles. Tonight, DeDe carried Jason as the pair flew through the woods.

"I must lodge a formal complaint. I do not think this is a good idea," Jason whined. A black blur appeared in front of them. "Tree!"

DeDe ducked under another large branch as she flew. "Oh, hush, you big baby," DeDe scolded. "Complaint noted."

"But the bugs," Jason complained as he tried to play on his friend's fear of insects. "I do not want to be eaten alive."

"Less whining, more moving," she kidded. "There is nothing to be afraid of. You won't get eaten alive."

"Says the nigh invulnerable one." Jason smiled. "Somehow if bullets bounce, then mosquitoes do not have a chance."

DeDe tried not to smile and failed.

After ducking under another branch, the duo had reached the end of the trail. The cemetery was directly in front of them. A large a chain-link fence blocked the way.

"We're there," DeDe whispered as she slowly floated to the ground. She pulled back the corner of the fence as she used her SkyVision to gaze across the cemetery. She did not see a single heat signature in the graveyard.

"Anyone there?" Jason asked as he squinted into darkness.

"It's dead out there," DeDe joked.

"Nice," Jason said sarcastically. He hated the cemetery at night.

"Quiet as a tomb," she added. DeDe loved pushing Jason's buttons. "Hey, you're the one who said I should work on my banter."

"You are not helping," Jason mumbled. No one answered. "DeDe?" he said in a loud whisper. "Where did you go?"

She was gone.

"A little warning next time. I did not even see you move."

Jason squinted through the fence into the graveyard. In the distance, he saw a DeDe-sized blur move across the cemetery to the location of her father's grave. "That is okay," he mumbled as he climbed from the woods and squeezed through the fence. "I will catch up." He climbed through the fence and looked around. "Through the dark and spooky graveyard." He took another step. "All alone."

#

On the other side of the cemetery, a black limousine pulled up to the front gate.

The rear door of the car opened to reveal a woman in flowing black robes with Greek symbols embossed on the sleeves in silver lettering. A purple rope cinched the robes around her waist, and held a matching small purple pouch. The woman's grey hair was pulled back in a tight bun, revealing the wrinkled features of Beatrice Tick, the Debole Academy's librarian.

She walked around to the other side of the car and faced the tinted window. She took a deep breath and spoke with an English accent, "I am ready, sir."

The window slowly dropped open with an electronic whine.

A deep voice spoke from inside the vehicle. "Remember the plan, Beatrice. We must obtain enough life force to accomplish the resurrection."

"I am certain that the Ressuructusscorpus spell will be sufficient for our needs," Beatrice said as she double-checked the contents of her pouch. "What rises will be mindless, but the creatures should gather more than enough energy to suit our needs."

"Our needs?" the man said angrily as he leaned into the open window. The moonlight revealed the familiar features of Principal Vilbran.

"Sorry, sir. I meant your needs."

"Very well, Miss Tick," Vilbran said with a sneer. "I will pick you up later and then see you tomorrow at the school to discuss the next part of the plan. I will come by the library."

"Thank you, sir. I will make some tea for us and show you our latest acquisitions. I have some lovely thirteenth century . . ." Beatrice looked up from her pouch, but the limo had already driven away. "Very well. I should be getting to work anyway."

Beatrice Tick turned to the front gate of the cemetery and raised her robed arms. The librarian began to chant in a strange, foreign tongue. Her hands glowed. Within moments, the glow spread up her arms and through her body. Soon, Miss Tick was engulfed in a bright yellow glow.

The glow became brighter and brighter.

\#

Jason was leaning up against a mausoleum with the name Kraus carved into the marble and sighing loudly.

Jason saw the flash of light out of the corner of his eyes. "What was that?" His words echoed off the marble mausoleums.

He rubbed his eyes and squinted as he looked across the cemetery grounds. Then he saw it: a bright, eerie glow emanating from behind the fence on the far side of the graveyard. "I sure hope that is a trick of the full moonlight's reflection." Jason looked up to the sky. The clouds had moved to completely conceal the moon. "That is, if there were any moonlight."

Jason grew concerned. He needed to find DeDe. He turned around and looked back towards where he thought his best friend might be, but with the moon gone, Jason couldn't see in the poorly lit cemetery. He fumbled in the dark. "DeDe? Are you there?"

A figure moved toward him in the darkness. Jason squinted into the dark cemetery to see it. He called out to his best friend, "DeDe, we have to go. There is something going on at the entrance on the other side of the cemetery."

The figure stood there and stared at him.

"Come on, now. Stop fooling around. This is not funny."

The figure still stood there silently.

Annoyed, Jason reached out to grab his friend's hand. "I am serious!"

Just then, a brisk breeze blew through the cemetery, and the clouds parted to reveal the full moon. The bright moonlight illuminated the cemetery, revealing what was in front of Jason's outstretched hand.

It was not DeDe.

Instead, a well-dressed, gaunt man with grey skin and glowing eyes that stared at him. Dirt covered the man's tuxedo, hands, and face. Jason looked past the man to see the hole in the ground and the casket that had been forced open from the inside.

After years of horror comics, Jason immediately recognized the situation. "Zombie!" he cried.

The man groaned an unintelligible response. Jason looked around the cemetery. The man was not alone. Several dozen people trudged slowly across the graveyard toward him. Others were clawing their way out of the cold earth. "I think we need a bigger boat." Jason murmured under his breath before he turned and ran towards DeDe.

Far away, DeDe sat on the ground in front of a large tombstone. She patted the dirt around some newly planted flowers and sighed. "I don't know what to do, Dad. Mike's a good guy, but I never thought he would marry mom."

She traced her fingers along the engraved inscription on the tombstone: *Beloved Father and Husband.* "On the bright side, I'm getting better with the power stuff and can even do that electronet thing, sort of." She felt tears well up in her eyes. "I wish you were here to help. It's hard sometimes." She couldn't fight it anymore. Tears ran down her face. "I really miss you, Daddy."

The sounds of running feet and Jason's screams interrupted her thoughts.

"DeDe! DeDe! DeDe!" he yelled as he threw her backpack at her. She quickly stood and wiped her eyes with one hand as she caught the airborne backpack with the other.

"What?" she asked, annoyed, and sniffled. "Can't I get a single moment of privacy?"

Jason gestured for her to look over his shoulder. There, she saw the creatures that slowly lumbered towards them.

"Um, what the heck are they?"

"Zombies!" he said excitedly.

"What did you do now?" DeDe asked with a sarcastic smile.

"Me? Why did I have to do something?"

"I don't know. Maybe because of -- you know -- the zombies." She opened her bag and pulled her purple and black costume from its secret compartment. "I'll be right back. Try not to do anything else while I'm gone."

"No, wait! Do not leave me," Jason pleaded.

But DeDe was gone in a blur of speed.

The closest zombie, the man in the tuxedo, had caught up to Jason. The creature groaned at the lanky teen.

Jason smiled in response. "Hi, Mr. Zombie man. Is there something I can do for you?"

The zombie answered by revealing his rotted teeth as he lunged towards Jason.

CHAPTER 39

As the Zombie reached out to grab him, Jason stared at the pale hand that moved toward him. Time seemed to stop, and he could see every detail with perfect accuracy. He saw the dirt under the creature's fingernails as they reflected in the light of the full moon. He wondered what the hand would feel like. Would it be cold and clammy or warm? It was a debate he had often had with his online community.

Jason never found out. Before the zombie could grab him, a headstone with the name *Siegel* on it flew through the air and slammed into the creature. The impact pulverized both the headstone and creature, turning them both into dust.

Jason turned around to see DeDe floating behind him. "Not DeDe," he corrected himself. "Sky Girl!" He watched her purple cape flutter in the night air as she floated above him. His best friend was quite an impressive sight.

Before he could say more, another creature growled and lumbered toward him.

Sky Girl landed next to Jason. "Any ideas?"

"Yeah, stomp your foot real hard!" Jason yelled.

"What?" Sky Girl asked, confused.

"Just do it! Stomp on the ground," Jason ordered. "Quick! Like one of your dance moves."

Sky Girl followed his instructions. The force of the impact tore the ground apart and knocked the creature into the newly opened grave.

"Cool!" Sky Girl said in amazement.

"I thought that might work," Jason said with a smile, "SkyBoy did it in the limited edition comic that came with the action figure of him in his silver spandex variant costume."

Sky Girl turned to her best friend. "You know, you have way too much free time. Wait a minute. That's huge. Why didn't you say something earlier."

"I know. I have a bunch of new things I want to try," Jason said hopefully. "Wait, what is huge?"

"That I'm allowed to change my costume!" Sky Girl beamed. "I thought I could only wear the one costume."

"You never asked, and I did not want to encourage you." Jason scanned the hundreds of creatures in the cemetery. "Listen, I do not think this is the time to talk about your wardrobe."

"Oh, please! There is never a bad time to talk about my wardrobe."

Jason gave her a scolding look.

Sky Girl brushed away a stray strand of hair that had fallen into her face. "Fine. What's the plan?"

Jason pointed to the opposite end of the cemetery. "I saw a glowing light over there before this whole thing started. I thought it was my imagination, but it may be the source of this. We should check it out and . . . ."

Before he could finish the sentence, Sky Girl scooped him up in her arms. The pair flew across the cemetery, over the fence, and landed outside the gated entrance to Colonia Memorial Gardens. She put Jason down.

"That was not too demeaning." Jason turned to his best friend. She had already placed her communication device in her right ear.

Jason examined the gate. A large padlock secured a thick chain that wrapped around it. "At least they cannot get out of the cemetery and into the town. That should buy us some time to figure this out. Hopefully they will not find our secret entrance in the back."

Sky Girl didn't respond.

He turned to look at her again. The color had drained from his best friend's face as she stared through the fence at something on the ground—a bird. Jason followed her gaze. The bird and several other animals lay lifeless on the ground.

"I think they're all dead," she said with a gasp. "There's no aura when I look at them with my SkyVision."

Jason glanced back at the two dozen zombies that had gathered on the other side of the fence. The creatures were putting pressure on the gate, but the lock held.

He pointed to the creatures. "What do you see when you look at them?"

Sky Girl focused her vision on the fence. "It's kind of weird. They have no heat signature at all; they're cold black. But some of them have green auras."

"Some of them?" Jason asked. "I wonder . . ."

Just then, a bird landed on one of the zombies, a pale woman in a plaid muumuu. The bird began to glow, and after a second, it fell to the floor, dead.

"She got a faint aura after she killed that bird," Sky Girl said in alarm. "I think she took it from him."

"I'm really glad you did not let that thing touch me," Jason said nervously.

"What do I do now?"

"You will do nothing but witness the triumph of MissTick!" a voice called from behind them.

Jason and Sky Girl spun around. MissTick stood on a rock outside of the cemetery, her arms outstretched, revealing the glowing mystical symbols on her robe. The sorceress glowed with power.

"We meet at last, Sky Girl!" The mage spoke with a modicum of disgust in her voice.

Jason stepped away into the shadows. He placed the microphone in his ear. With any luck, MissTick had not seen him. He tried to remember something about the villainess from the SkyBoy comics. He'd never really liked magical stories and hardly ever bought them.

"Sky Girl, I have no idea who this MissTick is," he whispered into the headset. "She must be pretty obscure. I have never heard of her." Jason examined the magician from the shadows, and though he wasn't completely sure, he thought there was something familiar about her.

Sky Girl stood confidently before the magician but murmured, "Great. I'm on my own." She raised her voice and addressed MissTick. "What did you do?"

The robed woman smiled. "The Ressuructusscorpus spell. And now my zombie army will absorb the town's life force."

Sky Girl turned to look at the zombies. The undead creatures pressed against the locked gate, piling up on each other in a feeble attempt to open the door. "I think you forgot about the gate." She turned back to MissTick. "The only place those creatures are going is back to their graves."

"I think not, Sky Girl!" MissTick raised her arm and pointed her finger at the metal entrance. A beam of light emerged from her hands and smashed into the gate. The beam pulverized and twisted the wrought iron, creating a large, gaping hole in the fence. One by one, the zombies began to squeeze out of the newly formed opening. The undead monsters streamed out onto the highway. Several of the creatures moved to attack Sky Girl, moaning as they lumbered toward her.

Sky Girl easily floated out of reach of the grasping zombies hands, laughing as the creatures reached for her. "You're going to have to do better than that."

"Very well. If you insist," MissTick laughed as she clasped her hands together and used her fingers to form a triangle. She gestured toward Sky Girl and opened her palms. "Now be quiet!" she roared.

Suddenly, Jason realized where he knew her from.

But it was too late. A blue beam emanated from MissTick's hands and smashed into Sky Girl. The force of the blast threw her back over the graveyard and into the night sky. As she flew through the air, Sky Girl tried to get her bearings in the darkness. But the ground quickly moved beneath her and appeared like a blur.

"Need to focus!" she cried out.

She closed her eyes and tried to create an electronet to break her fall. She thought of Adam and tried to feel the emotions build in her mind. Nothing happened. "I don't—" Sky Girl never finished her sentence. Instead, she slammed hard onto the grounds of a golf course about a mile away from the cemetery. The impact caused a small crater to form in a sand trap. Sky Girl struggled to lift her head. The golf course was next to the highway.

Sky Girl looked up to see the glowing sign that identified the gourmet restaurant known as La Sherrier. She had smashed into the ground right next to the place where Michael was going to propose to her mother.

"Um, sure. Why not? Not too ironic. Wait, did I actually just use ironic correctly? I must have hit the ground harder than I thought." Her head slumped into the dirt before she passed out with a groan.

#

Across town, Jason hid in an alleyway and watched as zombies streamed out of the cemetery. Luckily, the streets surrounding the cemetery were empty. He touched his microphone again. "Sky Girl, can you hear me?" There was no answer. Jason hoped she was okay. She'd been hit really hard.

He looked down the alleyway and onto the street. There was a 24-hour convenience store and a closed dry cleaner. The image of a hardware store reflected in the dry cleaner's windows. Jason watched as the monsters slowly filled the street. He tried to remember everything he had read about zombies. Most of the information was not very helpful. Don't get bitten. Hit them in the head, preferably with a double tap. Bury them with salt and silver. He looked at the hardware store again and smiled. "Could it be that easy?" He pressed the communicator one more time. "Sky Girl, please pick up. I have an idea."

#

Across town, Sky Girl still lay in the center of a large impact crater. Her communicator continued to beep in her ear. She did not answer it.

CHAPTER 40

"Oh, my head," Sky Girl said as she slowly opened her eyes.

As her vision focused, the costumed teen could see that she was in the Great Hall of the Galactic Protectorate. "Wonderful. Can this day get any worse?"

Sky Girl stood up and yelled into the room. "I have nothing to say to you guys. I'm just passing through, and now I'm leaving."

Her voice echoed off the chamber, and she immediately felt that something was wrong. Sky Girl looked around. The chamber was in ruins. Columns lay scattered across the floor. The council table was pulverized.

Sky Girl immediately took a defensive combat stance and prepared for battle. She focused her senses, and her SkyHearing picked up the sound of raspy breathing coming from under the marble council table. She used her SkyVision to examine the crumbled table and saw a red figure against the cold blue background. Sky Girl immediately recognized the shape of the figure.

"Boosadah!" she yelled as she rushed over and lifted the table off the lizard-like alien.

Boosadah's broken body lay under the table. Her red eyes were glassy, and she was covered in a sticky yellow substance that Sky Girl thought might be blood. The alien turned her head toward Sky Girl.

"Deidre," she said weakly. "You came."

DeDe took off her mask and wiped the tears that had formed in her eyes as she cradled the small, frail alien. "Who did this?" she choked.

"No time." Boosadah coughed up more of the sickly yellowish substance. "Last hope."

"Please don't die," DeDe cried softly.

"Father," Boosadah said with a gasp before her head dropped.

"What about my father?" DeDe focused her SkyVision on the alien and watched as her aura faded. Boosadah was gone.

The chamber was quiet.

DeDe began to cry. "No!" she sobbed repeatedly as she cradled the body of her former mentor. "No!"

DeDe heard a faint beeping, and the council chamber began fading away. Before it vanished, DeDe was sure she saw something purple and black moving toward her through the bright lights. She replaced her mask and closed her eyes tightly.

* * *

When Sky Girl opened her eyes again, she was still on the ground across the street from La Sherrier. She lifted herself from the ground slowly and staggered to a sitting position.

The communicator beeped in her ear. It was the beeping from the dream that had brought her back.

She touched a small activation button. "I'm here, Jason," she said sadly.

"Thank goodness," Jason responded in her ear. "Are you okay?"

Sky Girl thought of the lifeless body of Boosadah and how she'd watched the alien's aura fade. She wiped the tears away from her face with her gloved hand. "No, I am not okay. I'm really angry and want to hit something. Something happened with the Galactic Protectorate."

"It will have to wait. The zombies are moving toward the suburbs. I have a plan. But we need to move quickly."

"I'll be right there," Sky Girl promised as she rose to her feet. Before she could leave, the sound of laughter echoed across the golf course. She took off her mask, immediately recognizing the laughter as her mother's.

DeDe looked across the street and saw Michael and Dianne sitting at a table on the street. Heat lamps warmed the area as the two had an intimate dinner.

They were talking. Dianne was smiling. DeDe realized that she had only ever seen her mother smile like that in old photographs. In fact, DeDe hadn't remembered seeing her mother really smile since her dad had died. Dianne was truly happy now. And it was Michael that made her happy. DeDe smiled, too. She was sure Dianne still loved her father, but she was moving on with her life and had found someone to make her feel special. Someone who could make her feel the way DeDe's dad used to.

DeDe realized how selfish she had been. She stood in the sand pit and made a promise to accept Michael Valjorge into her life and family. Michael could never replace her father. But, he could be something new and good for her family.

The thought of her father brought to mind Boosadah's last words, but her thoughts were interrupted by Jason's urgent transmission.

"Sky Girl, I need you now!"

"Coming!" she yelled as she put her mask back on and jumped straight up into the air. Sky Girl streaked through the night sky back toward the cemetery.

Across the street, Michael reached into his coat and pulled out a small blue box as violinists gathered around Dianne.

CHAPTER 41

Five minutes earlier, Jason hid behind a green recycle bin and waited for the street to clear.

When the zombies were gone, he rushed out of the alleyway and across the road, quickly climbing the fence into the back lot of the hardware store. He winced in pain as his pants got caught in the barbed wire on the top of the fence. "Great." He sighed as he reached down and felt the gash on his leg. "That will leave a mark. I really need to be more active in gym class."

Jason limped around the yard in search of what he needed. Then he saw it sitting next to the fence -- a barrel labeled *melt-away*. He rushed over to the barrel and struggled to remove the lid. It came off with a loud cracking noise.

He peered in. The barrel was full of small white pellets. He took a moment to exhale in relief as he leaned against the fence.

He tried his communicator again. "I'm here, Jason." DeDe answered. Jason thought she sounded different; there was a mature sadness to her voice.

"Thank goodness." Jason responded. "Are you okay?"

Sky Girl responded in his ear "No, I am not okay. I'm really angry and want to hit something. Something happened with the Galactic Protectorate." Her voice began to crack. Jason needed her to focus.

"It will have to wait." Jason instructed. "The zombies are moving towards the suburbs." He looked over at the silver fencing piled up across the yard. "I have a plan. But we need to move quickly."

"I'll be right there."

Suddenly, the fence shook. Jason spun around to see a zombie reaching through it and grabbing where his head would had been if he had not ducked. The creature growled menacingly. Jason rolled away from the fence as the zombie, dressed in a dirty white tuxedo, ripped through the fence.

Jason touched his ear. "Sky Girl, I need you now!"

"Coming!" she said before the signal cut off.

The monster lunged towards Jason. He positioned the melt-away barrel between himself and the creature. Jason could see several other creatures stumbling through the newly made opening in the hardware store fencing.

"It's now or never." Jason reached into the barrel and grabbed a handful of the white powder. "Take that!" he yelled as he threw the powder at the zombie. The white dust landed on the creature's shoulders and covered its face.

The zombie looked concerned for a moment, but nothing happened.

Jason smile weakly at the creature. "So that went well."

The zombie growled and took a step forward. Suddenly, it began to smoke and dissolve. Jason stared in amazement as the creature evaporated, leaving nothing but a pile of dusty white clothes on the ground.

Jason turned to see four other zombies enter the yard. "Bring it on!" he yelled as he reached down to the ground to pick up a cup. He used it to scoop the white powder from the barrel.

Sky Girl flew over the yard moments later. Several piles of smoking clothing littered the yard, and Jason sat in the center of the yard surrounded by a circle of white powder.

There were a dozen zombies circling him. She was surprised that he seemed unconcerned with his predicament.

Jason looked up at his friend and smiled. "About time. I was getting bored."

"I see you made some friends. I hope you haven't replaced me as your best friend," Sky Girl said with smile. Beneath the smile, Jason could see the sadness in her eyes.

He winked and gestured to the creatures. "With these guys? No worries. They may look cool, but they are not very good conversationalists."

Sky Girl hovered and watched as one of the creatures tried to move toward Jason but stopped at the edge of the circle. "How did you . . .?"

Jason pointed at the ground. "Rock salt. It is made with silver nitrate. The undead always hated salt and silver in my old monster comics. As you can see, I was able to get a few," he said proudly and pointed at some empty clothing on the ground next to a barrel. "But then I got cut off from the barrel. So, I made a protective circle and waited for you. You got lost again, right?"

"Why am I not surprised that you found a way to stop them?" Sky Girl said as she landed in the middle of the circle. She hugged her friend, who winced in pain. Jason's pant leg was soaked with blood. "You're hurt."

"It is just a flesh wound," he said with a thick Cockney accent and smiled.

DeDe thought of Boosadah. She could not lose anyone else tonight. "I've got to get you to a hospital."

Jason held up his hand. "First we have to stop MissTick's zombie army before they can destroy the town by draining everyone's life force." He paused for a moment and smiled. "Do you find it odd that that this stuff does not sound strange to us anymore?"

"You are such a geek."

"Speaking of geeks," he said seriously, "I finally remembered where I saw her. I think MissTick is the school librarian. I went to check, but she disappeared after knocking you across town."

"So that is two chemistry teachers, an English teacher, and now the school librarian. I tell you, the Debole Academy needs to do better background checks." Sky Girl adjusted her purple cape and smiled. "No wonder Nicole wanted to go there so badly."

She looked across the yard at the growing number of zombies that were gathering in the streets of Colonia.

"She raised the whole cemetery. We do not have much time," Jason said with concern.

Sky Girl put her hands on her hips and lowered her voice one octave. "Give me the plan."

CHAPTER 42

MissTick stood outside the cemetery gates, pacing back and forth across the opening. She checked her watch again and squinted into the dark, but she saw nothing.

Finally, a dark limousine pulled up alongside the librarian. MissTick nervously opened the door and climbed in taking the seat across from Principal Vilbran.

"I trust you were successful," Vilbran said with a scowl.

"I do not know," she replied quietly.

"You do not know?"

"I sent the zombie army out to obtain the life force."

"And?" Vilbran asked with annoyance.

"I lost them."

"All of them?" he yelled.

"Nearly three hundred, yes, sir." She lowered her eyes in shame. "They never came back."

Vilbran stared out the window. "Sky Girl!" He said the words like a curse.

"No, sir," MissTick volunteered. "She and Mr. Shewstal showed up earlier. I used the pushstal spell to get rid of her. She cannot possibly still be a problem."

"Mr. Shewstal?" Vilbran asked calmly. "Sky Girl was with Mr. Shewstal?"

"Oh, yes. He tried to hide, but I saw him." She tapped the side of her head. "Librarian eyes do not miss much."

Vilbran moved across the seat and slapped the librarian hard across the face. "You find the missing clue to the identity of our arch nemesis, and you do not bother to mention it?"

MissTick stared in shock at Vilbran for a moment. A large red welt began to show on her cheek. "But I thought. . ."

"No, you did not think. Now go," Vilbran said calmly, pointing to the door of the limo.

"But—" MissTick attempted to explain.

"Go get your zombies and bring them back."

MissTick paused for a moment. "Yes sir." She placed her hand on the door handle.

Vilbran placed his hand on top of hers. "Or do not come back at all. Beatrice, I mean it." He let her go.

After a moment, he reached for the car phone and dialed. The call connected, and a young woman answered.

"Miss Backerchase. Prepare for me. I am coming to your home. I also need you to go to the school and pull two students' files for me." There was silence on the other end of the line. "I need the personal files for Mr. Jason Shewstal and Miss Diedre Christopher. I think they will prove interesting nighttime reading."

Vilbran hung up the phone and laughed maniacally.

MissTick heard the laughter as she watched the car pull away. After a moment, the mystic started down the long road into town to see what had happened to her zombies.

#

Across town, Jason and Sky Girl stood outside the large fenced-in area. Jason examined the container again.

"I think that will hold them," he said with pride. "And you thought my zombie movies were dumb."

A few minutes earlier, he had outlined his grand plan. Using the silver fencing, he had Sky Girl make a containment area. Jason had read that zombies were vulnerable to pure silver as well as salt. Logically, he assumed a silver fence could contain the monsters.

Next, he had Sky Girl pick up the dumpster in the alleyway. She used it scoop up all the zombies and place them in the makeshift pen. Of course, he'd had to first make sure there were no bugs in the dumpster. DeDe was afraid of bugs. Jason smiled. Since she had obtained her powers, she had faced two giant mechanical robots, a genie, a demon, and now, magical zombies. Superpowers or not, a small bug could send his best friend screaming across the room.

"What are you smiling about?" Sky Girl asked as she picked up another bag of salt.

"Nothing." Jason decided the irony would be lost on Sky Girl. "Okay, it is time to implement the final stage of our endeavor."

"Huh?" DeDe asked, momentarily losing her Sky Girl voice.

"Just fly over and dump the rock salt on them."

Sky Girl lowered her voice an octave and winked through her purple mask. "Oh, why didn't you say so? I'm off."

She floated above the corner of the cage and sprinkled the rock salt on a zombie dressed in a pale white Hawaiian shirt. "Seriously, I wouldn't be caught dead in that shirt," she said with a giggle.

Jason rolled his eyes. "Please do not mock the dead guy." He did agree, however, that it was an incredibly ugly shirt.

The salt sprinkled down on the creature, which began to smoke as it took effect. A few seconds later, the only thing that remained on the ground was a smoldering Hawaiian shirt and tan pants.

"It worked!" Jason said with a mix of excitement and relief. "You should hurry up if we want to get rid of the rest by morning. By daybreak, there will be nothing but clothing out here."

"Maybe we can have a garage sale or something," Sky Girl joked as she flew over another zombie. "Or donate them all to Goodwi—"

Sky Girl was unable to finish her sentence. Instead, the young heroine screamed in pain as a bolt of lightning struck her from behind. Her electrified body lit up the night sky as her screams filled the air.

Sky Girl dropped the bag of salt, which fell harmlessly into the center of the holding pen.

"Sky Girl!" Jason screamed. It looked as if she was being electrocuted. He knew that was impossible; DeDe was immune to electricity. They had tested it out over the summer. It had to have been something else. Jason scanned the ground for the cause of his friend's agony. No one was on the street.

Sky Girl writhed in pain as she floated above the pen, screaming in agony. Her red hair floated in the air, suspended by the statically electrified air.

"Jason, help me!" she finally screamed.

"I . . ." Jason was speechless. He did not know how much more abuse his best friend could take. He scanned the rooftops and looked up at the top of the fence. That's where Jason saw the cause of his friend's pain.

MissTick had climbed up the silver fencing and was standing on the top corner of the enclosure. She had her arms outstretched toward Sky Girl. The librarian's eyes were closed, and her mouth was moving. Jason could not make out the words but assumed she was casting some sort of spell.

He ran toward the fence at a sprint, but the pain in his leg forced him to run with a limp. He tried to ignore the burning agony in his leg. "I have to get to the fence and do something."

Of course, he had no idea what he would do when he got there.

Sky Girl screamed louder. Jason looked up to see smoke emanating from her body. He feared for his friend's life.

Preoccupied with his friend's predicament, he failed to judge the distance to the fence as he ran in the dark. He slammed face first into the corner of the metal fence with full force. Stunned, he fell back to the ground.

The force of Jason's impact shook the whole fence, knocking MissTick off balance. The sorceress opened her eyes and tried to regain her footing, but the fence continued to wobble beneath her feet.

With MissTick distracted, her spell was broken. Sky Girl stopped glowing and fell limply into the center of the enclosure. Several zombies lumbered toward the wounded heroine. Sky Girl struggled to get to her feet and failed.

On the other side of the fence, MissTick screamed as she fell hard onto several zombies. The force of the landing knocked the wind out of MissTick, leaving her unable to cast any spells. She screamed in terror as one of the creatures reached around and grabbed her face. Just as the others had done with the birds, the creature began to drain the life force from her.

"DeDe, look out!" Jason screamed as a zombie in a black dress reached out to touch her. Sky Girl tried to get up but slumped back to the ground.

Jason glanced over at MissTick. The glowing mage screamed, "Get away!" as she vanished beneath a horde of zombies.

Unable to look away from the carnage, Jason would remember the sound of her screams for the rest of his life.

Suddenly, a bright golden light appeared in the center of the horde. The light spread out in a circle and washed over the zombies nearest to the librarian. As the light touched each zombie, the creatures vanished in a flash. The light expanded to cover the entire enclosure. The zombie in the black dress dissolved just as it was about to touch Sky Girl. She rolled over on her back and sighed in relief.

"That was good thinking, knocking her into the zombie pit," Sky Girl said weakly from her prone position.

"Yeah, good thinking," Jason said as he lay on the ground on the other side of the fence. He rubbed his face and head where a large welt was forming. "All part of my plan."

CHAPTER 43

Jason limped through the open glass door to DeDe's house. He hobbled over to the basement bathroom, turned on the light, and entered DeDe's purple lavatory.

As he washed the dried blood from his face, he watched the pink water swirl down the drain. Jason examined his nose, hoping it wasn't broken.

"I have got to get a healing power," he said with a wince as he looked at his face in the bathroom mirror. "I look horrible." His nose was puffy, and it looked like he had the beginnings of two black eyes. He wondered what Angela Leary and Penny Pound would think of these latest battle scars. He made a tough guy face. "Hey, babe. Scars are just tattoos with character." That thought made him smile. Unfortunately, even smiling hurt, so he stopped.

Jason opened the medicine cabinet and took out some hydrogen peroxide. He sat on the floor and rolled up his jeans to reveal the gash on his leg, opened the bottle, and poured the clear liquid on the cut. "Wowza, that hurt!" He sat up quickly and slammed his head on the sink. "Oh, come on!" he yelled to no one in particular.

Ten minutes later, Jason's cut was bandaged. His face almost looked presentable, but the bump on his head was beginning to throb.

As he exited the bathroom, he heard the front door open.

"DeDe, is that you?" he called. "Where did you go?" He walked up the stairs, immediately realizing his error when he came face to face with Dianne and Michael.

"Where did who go?" Dianne asked with annoyance.

"Hello, Mrs. Christopher, Mr. Valjorge," Jason stammered. "Um, where did what go? Wow, is that an engagement ring?"

Dianne, still annoyed, could not help but smile. "Why, yes it is, Jason."

"Can I see it?" Jason walked up into the light to see the ring. "Wow. Congratulations!"

Dianne stared at the ring for a moment. "Thank you." She seemed to catch on. "But don't change the subject. Where is my daughter?" She turned to give Jason a stern look but gasped when she saw his bruises. "What happened to your face?"

"My face?" Jason asked innocently. "Did something happen to my face?"

Just then, there was a noise from the upstairs ceiling. "I found it!" DeDe yelled from the stairs that led to the attic of 16 Hartland Court. Jason and Dianne turned to look up the stairs. DeDe came down the portable ladder that extended from the attic into the second floor hallway. She held a small white pouch in her hand. "I knew I had an extra ice pack with my old softball gear." Dressed in sweatpants and a Les Misérables t-shirt, DeDe entered the foyer with an embarrassed smile.

"I was showing Jason some new high kicks and, um, kicked too high. Like kick-you-in-the-face high." She put the ice pack on Jason's nose. "Sorry."

Jason smiled and moved the ice pack to his head with a wince. "Thanks. Your Mom thought you had gone out."

"Oh, yeah, and I flew up on the roof and climbed into the attic so you couldn't see me." She gave Jason a secret wink. Mr. Valjorge watched with interest.

"So, how was dinner?" DeDe asked her mother. "Did you say yes to Mr. Valjorge?"

Dianne held out her hand. "We're getting married!" she said excitedly.

Jason paused, waiting for one of the dramatic explosive rants DeDe had been rehearsing all night.

It never came. Instead, she squealed with delight and hugged her mother.

"I'm so happy for you both," she said with tears in her eyes.

"You'd better be," Dianne said, her own eyes tearing up. "I want my baby to be in the wedding party."

"Mom!" DeDe protested as she pulled away. "I'm a little too old to be a flower girl."

Dianne laughed. "No, dummy, as my maid of honor."

"Really?" DeDe started to cry again as she hugged her mother again. "I accept. I accept."

Jason decided that it was a good time to sneak out. He went down the stairs to get his backpack and turned to the glass door to head home.

"Jason, wait a minute," DeDe called from upstairs. She rushed down to catch him.

"Nice save up there with the whole ice pack thing," Jason said as he sat down on the couch. "You are getting much better at covering your secret identity. I am proud of you." He winced in pain as he sat.

"Are you really okay?" DeDe asked as she sat next to him. "That leg looks really bad."

"I'll tell mom I fell on the way home and need to go to the doctor. Maybe I can get even out of gym class for a while."

They both laughed.

Jason took a more serious tone. "I was more worried about you. MissTick really did a number on you."

DeDe lowered her voice to a whisper. "I've never felt so much pain. I thought I was nigh invulne . . . involun . . . oh, whatevs."

"Invulnerable," he corrected with a smile. "We will have to figure it out. I do not remember if SkyBoy was vulnerable to magic. Maybe you are just not invulnerable to it."

"Well, it really hurt," DeDe said. "The same thing happened with Genie D-Man."

Jason smiled. "Just to be safe, we had better not go to any magic shows until we figure this out." Then his voice turned serious. "Where did you go after the fight?"

"That's what I wanted to talk to you about. Something happened." DeDe's eyes watered, and her voice began to crack. "First, Boosadah is dead,"

Jason moved to her side and hugged her. After a moment, she composed herself and was able to continue.

"When MissTick knocked me out, I woke up in the Hall of the Galactic Protectorate. The place was destroyed. Boosadah was trapped under a marble table. I—" She buried her head on Jason's shoulder and sobbed. "Jason, she died in my arms, and I couldn't do anything."

"Do we know who did it?" Jason asked softly, trying to not upset her further.

She shook her head in the negative. "Somebody was there, but I didn't—I couldn't. . . " Grief overcame her, and she couldn't continue. DeDe sobbed uncontrollably.

Jason held her and let her cry.

When the tears were gone, DeDe moved to her side of the couch and continued her story. "I woke up outside the restaurant. Mom looked so happy. Mr. Valjorge makes her happy. I can't stand in the way of that."

Jason nodded and took her hand. "That is very mature of you." It certainly explained her change in attitude.

"I have my moments." DeDe cleared her throat. "So I had a lot to think about. After MissTick vanished and I got you here, I flew back to the cemetery." She cleared her throat again.

Jason squeezed her hand. "Take your time."

"No, it's okay. So when I got to the cemetery, the place was a mess; the ground was all torn up."

"I would guess so. Miss Tick resurrected the entire cemetery."

"I know. So that's why I had to see my dad's grave."

"Oh, DeDe," Jason said sympathetically. He could only have imagined what had happened when DeDe showed up at her father's graveside. "How bad was it?"

DeDe stood up and turned to face Jason. "You don't understand. The whole cemetery was ripped apart. The ground was disturbed, and there were holes everywhere. Every grave was forced open as those—creatures rose to do MissTick's bidding. Every grave, that is, except my dad's. His was perfectly fine."

"Really?" Jason asked in shock. "Maybe MissTick just missed one. Or the fact that he was SkyBoy made him immune to her power."

"That's what I thought. So I dug up my father's grave," she said matter-of-factly.

"You dug it up?" Jason exclaimed. He pictured his friend as a wild-eyed grave digger. "You dug up your father's grave?"

"Yep," DeDe replied with a smile. "And you know what? It was empty."

"Empty?" Jason exclaimed. "Your father's grave was empty!"

"Shush. Mom will hear."

"I forgot," he whispered. "It was really empty?"

"Completely empty."

DeDe grinned.

"I think my Dad is still alive."

To Be Continued.

Sky Girl Will Return
In

Sky Girl and the Superheroic Return

Sky Girl and the Superheroic Return Preview

Sky Girl carried Jason through the dark night. Jason was exhausted, but excited. He peered out into the blackness but the teen could not see a thing. Far below him, he could hear the sounds of the Pacific Ocean as the waves rolled crashing against each other.

"Are you sure we're going the right way?" Sky Girl asked, impatiently.

Jason hit the button on the small GPS device and the screen lit up. As the only source of illumination in the blackness, the small screen blazed like a small sun. It took a moment for Jason's eyes to adjust to the brightness. He looked at the readout on the map and reported, "We are ten miles off the coast of China. Just keep going straight and you cannot miss it."

Jason looked down and peered into the inky black water. Even with the added light from the device, he could not see anything below him. He took a deep breath and added. "Are you doing okay? You are not. ."

"I'm not going to drop you." Sky Girl interrupted. Jason had asked the question more than a dozen times since they started their journey.

"Just checking." Jason was amazed at his best friend's stamina. They had been flying for over 4 hours and she did not even appear tired.

"Hold on. I'm going to try to make up some time." Sky Girl warned.

Jason carefully placed the device in the backpack tied around his waist and put down the visor to the motorcycle helmet. "Ok, ready." He took a deep breath and held it. He felt the wind rush his face as Sky Girl accelerated. Jason had learned earlier that it was impossible for him to breath at such speeds. He hoped the motorcycle helmet would prevent windburn, just as his coveralls cut down on wind resistance and friction. Still, he could feel the heat through the heavy insulation. Not for the first time on this trip, he wished he had Sky Girl's invulnerability.

Minutes later, they landed on the Chinese shoreline. The sun began to rise. Jason took off his helmet and took in the beautiful dawn. "Wow, look at that."

"We don't have time to take in the sites." She reached for the bag and took out the device. Her hands were shaking.

Jason took his friends hands and looked into her mask covered eyes. "DeDe, take a deep breath and relax."

Sky Girl closed her eyes and took a deep centering breath. "Sorry. It's just . . ."

"I know." he said as he took the device from her hands and looked at it. 20 hours remained before the deadline. He added, "It is going to be okay. Besides, we are way ahead of schedule."

"Thanks to you." Sky Girl smiled. Even at SkySpeed, they knew that Sky Girl could never reach China in time.

Jason knew he needed to come up with a solution.

That's when Jason remembered an experimental airline he read about online. Theoretically, these new planes would not fly straight from point to point. Instead, the ship arced into the upper atmosphere at an angle, thus using the revolution of the planet to speed up the trip.

After performing some complicated geometry, Jason had Sky Girl fly up into the upper atmosphere at a 48 degree angle. They then continued their arc down to earth.

Of course, Jason did not tell DeDe about the risks he took by flying into the upper atmosphere without a spaceship or spacesuit. However, since SkyBoy had regularly carried Dianne into space, Jason gambled that Sky Girl's aura would somehow protect him from the rigorous of reentry and allow him to breath.

For the most part, Jason's plan worked. They had traveled the 6,945 miles from North America to Asia in under 3 hours.

"See, math is fun." Jason smiled. He did feel a little guilty. He had slightly misjudged the angle and they missed the target by over fifty miles. "I recalculated. It will be quicker on the way back. I promise." Jason made a mental note and adjusted the angle for the return trip.

Sky Girl brushed the hair from her face and smiled. "My little nerd." She teased.

Jason checked their position. "The village is five klicks to the south east."

"Five what?" Sky Girl asked in confusion.

"Klicks."

"Hunh? What's a 'Klick'?"

Jason rolled his eyes, "Klick, it is short for kilometer."

"Then why didn't you just say 'kilometer'?" Sky Girl asked in response.

"Because saying 'klick' is way cooler."

Sky Girl just glared at him.

Finally, Jason sighed, "Fine. It is five kilometers that way." He pointed into the distance.

Sky Girl followed his finger and concentrated. "I see it." Before Jason could speak again, she scooped him up and flew towards the village. Jason watched as the trees went by at SkySpeed. It was like watching a movie in played at fast forward, in a really warm theater.

Seconds later, they were outside a small fishing village. Thatch roofs covered bamboo walls. The sand covered streets were littered with fishing equipment and cooking paraphernalia. Several poles on the outskirts of the village were ornately decorated with carvings of symbols that resembled the Choyut Dragon.

Jason took a deep breath as he put on one of DeDe's masks. Sky Girl thought he looked kind of silly but did not want to hurt his feelings. "Are you ready?" She asked.

Jason spoke with determination. "Let us do this." He spoke in a deep gravelly voice.

"What is that?" Sky Girl asked with a laugh.

"What is what?" Jason asked in his harsh voice.

"Your voice." Sky Girl smiled. "You know." She tried to mimic his gravelly tone, "your voice."

"It is my vigilante voice." Jason explained in deep tones. For effect, he added, "I am the dark."

"You are the dork?" She chuckled.

Jason pouted. "Not the dork, the dark." He lowered his voice deeper, "I am the night!"

"Oh, you are something." Sky Girl chided.

Jason resumed his normal voice. "Fine, we should just go."

Sky Girl put her hand on his shoulder. "No, really, use the voice. I think you should."

Jason replied in his gravelly tone, "Really, you like it?"

Sky Girl gave him a wink. "Yeah, I think it's cute."

Jason took his friends gloved hand and rolled his eyes. "Just move."

The two figures snuck into the village.

Neither of them noticed the group of costumed individuals following them.

ABOUT THE AUTHOR

Joe Sergi is a life-long comic fan who lives outside of Washington, DC with his wife and daughter. Joe is an attorney and a Haller Award winning author who has written articles, novels, short stories, and comic books in the horror, scifi, and young adult genres. His first novel, *Sky Girl and the Superheroic Legacy* was selected Best of 2010 by the New PODler Review. In addition, Joe will be releasing two books from McFarland Press, *Great Zombies in History* and *Comic Book Law for the Comics Creator*, in 2013. When not writing, Joe works as a Senior Litigation Counsel in an unnamed US government agency and is a member of the adjunct faculty at George Mason University School of Law.